An Elemental Earth

Ardraci Elementals, Book 4

Carol R. Ward

An Elemental Earth
Copyright 2017 by Carol R. Ward
Published by Brazen Snake Books

To Karin Eider,
whose idea it was to keep the fire going.

Acknowledgments

A special thank you to my daughter, Ciara Ward-Baker, for the hours she put in to produce such an awesome cover. And to Jamie DeBree, for all of her hard work on everything else.

Chapter One

The seeker-class scout ship seemed minuscule in comparison to the firefighter starship it shot out of, but for Zephryn it was the perfect size. While it could comfortably hold five people if need be, it was perfect for just one. Or in this case, two.

"Now that we're underway, can you share what exactly it is we're looking for?" he asked the small, grey being in the seat beside his.

"You will know it when you see it. Keep to the co-ordinates I have entered into the navigational computer."

Zephryn sighed. He should have known better than to expect a straight answer from Da'nat. Most of the Ilezie he'd met were the same way, never answering a question directly when they could couch it in mysteries and riddles. They could be quite an annoying species at times.

"I find it most interesting that you enjoy the vastness of space so much."

Zephryn tore his gaze away from the stars streaming past to glance at his companion. "Why is that?"

"Most of those liberated from Dr. Arjun's compound have

displayed varying degrees of agoraphobia, yet you seek out the open spaces."

Shrugging, Zephryn faced the stars again. "Space has always fascinated me. All my independent studies when I was growing up had to do with space and flight."

Growing up in a compound, product of an illicit breeding program, there had been little to occupy himself with except studies. The information they had access to was strictly controlled, and they weren't encouraged to socialize. But now that he was free he could finally live the life he dreamed of.

* * * * *

As the days passed with no change in course, Zephryn felt as though his curiosity would eat him alive. He passed the time exercising and watching vid-cubes, sometimes just sitting in front of the view port watching the stars stream by.

The tiny hold of the ship was filled with scientific equipment, most of which was unfamiliar to him, but when he asked Da'nat about it he was simply told, "It's Ilezie. Don't touch any of it."

Da'nat spent most of his time in meditation.

They were twelve days out when Zephyrn recognized where they were headed.

"Do you realize you have us going straight to the Deadlands?"

He wasn't sure whether to be excited or apprehensive. The Deadlands was an area of space that was devoid of pretty much anything except minerals. The Mining Guild laid claim to it and didn't appreciate outsiders. On the one hand, it was a dangerous place to travel to. But on the other hand, the explorer in him relished the adventure of it.

Da'nat checked the navigational computer. "You are correct. We will be entering the Deadlands to reach our target."

"What is our target?" Zephryn asked impatiently.

"That." The Ilezie pointed a long, boney, grey finger towards the front view screen.

Zephryn squinted his eyes. There was definitely something ahead of them, barely discernible but rapidly growing larger as they hurtled towards it.

"What is that?"

"It is elemental energy," Da'nat said, a note of awe in his voice. It was that note that had Zephryn looking at him in astonishment.

"But—"

"You need to bring us as close to it as possible."

"But—"

"There are things about it . . . so much is unknown. It is a phenomena that should not be possible, and yet it was predicted generations ago. We did not know we would be the instrument of our own—" The Ilezie broke off whatever it was he was about to say.

The object was shaped like a comet - a rough ball with tail streaking behind it. As they drew closer Zephryn activated the forward shields to protect their eyes from its brightness. It was a brilliant white, threaded with streaks of blue, green and yellow.

"Where did it come from?" Zephryn asked.

"It is the product of—"

The little ship shook as an energy burst hit them. Whatever the Ilezie was going to say was drowned out by the sound of alarms.

"Hang on!" Zephryn yelled. He fought with the controls of the ship. The inertial dampeners were off line, the electrical system was failing. "I hope there's a planet close by; we're going down!"

* * * * *

Chloe sat up with a start, not sure what had awakened her. Something wasn't right. Something . . .

Throwing off her covers, she got out of bed and padded barefoot down the short hall to her mother's room. Everything seemed in order - Tierra did not appear to be in distress although her breathing seemed somewhat erratic.

As Chloe stood trying to decide whether she should wake her mother for a dose of the precious medicine, a hand shot out from beneath the covers to grip her arm.

"A ship!" Tierra's eyes were fever bright as she looked up at her daughter. "There is a ship. You must save him!"

"Save who?" Chloe asked, startled.

"He can save you as well," her mother told her. "You must find him!"

"Mother, you've been dreaming, that's all. No one ever comes to this world without authorization," Chloe told her in a soothing voice.

Tierra's grip tightened. "This is not a dream! Reach out - can you not feel the wound to the earth?"

To humour her mother so she'd go back to sleep, Chloe reached out with her senses. "There's—" Her eyes widened. "I feel it! Something has impacted the surface."

"You must go and save him."

"Me? Why me? And save who? Wouldn't it be better to—"

"No! It must be you. Promise me!"

"All right, all right. I'll go. But you need to calm down. Whatever this is it's not worth making yourself more ill than you already are."

"Gannon must not find him, or his ship." Tierra's eyes began to close and her grip loosened.

Chloe disengaged herself gently and tucked her mother's arm beneath the covers again. She had half a mind to just go back to bed herself, but she couldn't afford for her mother to become more agitated about whatever was going on. She'd take a quick look around, and when she proved to herself, and her mother, it was nothing but a stray meteor that had somehow managed to slip through the protection grid, she could return home with a clear conscience.

With a sigh, she went back to her room to get dressed.

* * * * *

The night air was cold, but the two moons provided enough light for Chloe to see where she was going. There was no danger of running into any search party Gannon might send out. He'd be working with sensors and radar maps, while she followed the path provided by the land itself.

It did not take her long to find the place where the object had struck. There was a long gash in the earth ending in a smoking hollow. Within the hollow was a ship - a ship unlike any Chloe had ever seen before. This was no mining vessel!

Filled with a sense of urgency she did not understand, she scrambled down into the hollow and located the hatch of the vessel. It opened easily beneath her touch and she hesitated before entering.

"Hello?" she called. "Are you all right in there?"

There was no answer, but the sense of urgency increased. Catching her bottom lip between her teeth, she cautiously entered. Dim lights came on as the door slid shut behind her, making her jump.

"Hello?" she called again. There was still no answer and she moved slowly towards the front of the craft. The short passage had several doors, but instinctively she knew what she sought was behind the door at its end.

It slid open automatically and she found the pilot, unconscious and still strapped into his seat. Chloe cursed under her breath. It was obvious he was larger than she was, how was she supposed to get him out of the ship, let alone away from here before Gannon arrived?

Anti-grav sled, a voice whispered in her mind.

Startled, she glanced around. "Who said that?"

Aft compartment.

The sense of urgency was almost unbearable. Chloe quickly left the cockpit and hurried to the aft compartment where she found the anti-grav sled that was used for moving heavy cargo. Towing it behind her, she returned to the front where she managed to free the pilot from his restraints and push him out of his seat and onto the sled.

"Sorry," she said, wincing in sympathy as he hit the sled hard. There wasn't a sound out of him. She really hoped she hadn't added to his injuries.

The sled moved easily behind her, although she had to take

an angled path out of the hollow to keep her passenger from sliding off. The sense of urgency increased as she saw lights tracing a grid like pattern in the distance. As she topped the rise just above the crash site, Chloe heard the voice again.

Conceal the ship.

"Mother?" she asked in a whisper, remembering Tierra telling her that Gannon must not find either the pilot or the ship.

Protect the ship.

Chloe turned to face the ship. Moonlight reflected in her eyes as they changed from brown to green and back again as she concentrated. The earth around the ship shivered and the ship slowly sank downwards. Once it was several feet below the surface, the gash in the earth repaired itself.

As Chloe faced forward and began dragging the sled behind her towards home, grass and weeds began growing in the bare earth where the gash had been. Plants sprang up behind her, covering her tracks away from the site.

Chapter Two

Zephryn made a noise as he came awake. It was not as manly as a groan, but he refused to believe the involuntary sound that escaped him was as girly as a moan. His head hurt. So did his chest. And as he became more aware, a myriad of smaller aches and pains made themselves known.

He stopped trying to move and blinked several times, trying to get his vision to clear. A frown furrowed his brow. All he could see was green. Granted it was a soothing shade of green, but it definitely wasn't his cabin on the ship. Where was he?

More importantly, where was his ship? He had definitely been on his ship. Da'nat had been with him. They'd been on a mission, a mission to . . . what?

Air hissed between his teeth as he levered himself up to a sitting position. They'd been on some mysterious mission following a glowing ball of energy through space. Da'nat had been acting very strangely, and then the energy ball had . . . attacked them.

He remembered fighting with the controls of the scout ship, but he didn't remember landing. Obviously he'd landed safely though.

"Da'nat?" he called tentatively, not really expecting an answer.

The room he was in was small, holding only the bed he was in, a dresser, a small table beside the bed, and a chair that had clothes draped over it. Zephryn's eyes widened and he lifted up the blanket covering him for confirmation. The clothes on the chair were *his* clothes.

As he opened his mouth to call for Da'nat again, someone stepped through the open door. Zephryn's mouth shut with a snap. It was a woman, dressed in nothing but a dark brown towel. Another smaller towel was wrapped around her head. He couldn't have stopped the slow smile that slid across his face if he tried.

"Hello," he said.

She let out a squeak and jumped, nearly losing her grip on the towel.

"Oh! You're awake. I'm sorry, I didn't expect you to wake up so soon. I just—" she pulled clothing out of the dresser at random. "I'll be right back," she said, and fled the room.

Zephryn's grin widened and he moved himself into a more comfortable seated position in the bed while he waited for her to return. This could be interesting. Very interesting indeed.

She was quicker than he expected, and he was disappointed to see she was fully dressed in a pair of dark trousers and a shapeless brown shirt. Her hair was pulled back and neatly confined, still dark with dampness. He guessed the colour would be a coppery brown when it was dry. But though she was able to hide her body, there was no hiding her face. She was the most beautiful woman he'd ever seen.

"How are you feeling?" she asked, staying in the doorway.

Even her voice was beautiful, low and husky, sending a shiver right down to his groin.

"A little sore," he admitted, "But I think I'll live. Where am I?"

"You're in the Righteous Angels mining colony on Belspar. Do you remember what happened to you?"

"Yes, I crashed," he said ruefully. All at once he remembered Da'nat, but as he opened his mouth to ask about the Ilezie, a voice filled his head.

Do not tell her about me, it commanded. *And do not tell her what we were doing in this region of space.*

Da'nat? Zephryn projected with his mind. *Is that you?*

Of course it is me, who else would be bothered to waste their energy communicating with you.

"What about my ship, is it all right?" Zephryn asked instead.

She shrugged. "It appeared to be intact, but I know nothing about the inner workings of such things."

"What is your name?" they asked at the same time.

Blushing, she looked at the ground. "Chloe," she said.

"A beautiful name," he told her, causing her blush to deepen. "I'm Zephryn, Chloe. Were you the one who pulled me from my ship?"

"I—yes, that was me. I used the anti-grav sled from your ship to bring you here. I wasn't sure how seriously you were hurt — you'll have a bruise across your chest from slamming into the restraint, but other than that …"

Her voice trailed off and she was having a hard time meeting his eyes. He found her shyness utterly endearing.

"Thank you for rescuing me, Chloe," he said. "I seem to be

all right, except for my head." He reached up, wincing as he touched a bruised area.

"You seem to have an unaccountably hard head," she said with flicker of a smile. "If it's bad I can send for Granny."

"No need to trouble your granny, the pain's already fading."

"She's not *my* granny, she's just Granny. She's the closest thing to a healer we have without having to see the mine doctor. She sits with my mother when I have to work in the mine."

"You work in a mine?" he repeated, not sure he heard correctly. How could anyone put such a delicate creature to work in a mine?

"Just about everyone works in the mines on Belspar," she told him. "It's all there is. I left some broth simmering for when you awakened. I'll go fetch you some," she said abruptly. And with that she was gone again.

Zephryn stared after her, bemused.

I can see where this is going to be quite the struggle to get you to pay attention to the task at hand. Da'nat's voice in his mind was filled with a touch of amusement.

* * * * *

Chloe pressed her hands to her warm cheeks, trying to will the flush to go away. She couldn't believe the handsome stranger had caught her wearing nothing but a towel! And what was he doing awake anyway? By rights he should have been unconscious for at least another day.

Her face flamed anew as she remembered the struggle to undress him. It wasn't that she'd never seen a naked man before, it was just … he was so beautiful. But she'd had to check to make sure he had no other injuries, and then it just made sense to remove his flight suit completely so she could wash the blood off of it.

And now that beautiful, very naked man, was awake and in her bed. She'd never be able to sleep in that bed again without thinking of him.

Grinning at her fanciful notion, she continued on to the kitchen to fetch the broth. Her smile faded though as she realized it would be best if she did not acquire any romantic notions about him. It was too dangerous, not just for her, but mostly for him.

It was just as well he'd awakened early, she wouldn't have to worry about him wandering off while she was in the mines tomorrow. But now that he was awake, what was she supposed to do with him? How long were they going to be able to keep him hidden from Gannon? She wished her mother would wake up and tell her what to do. This had been her idea in the first place.

She arranged a bowl filled with broth and a couple of thick slices of the bread she'd baked that morning onto a tray and carried it back to her room. The stranger, Zephryn, had a pillow propped up behind him and was leaning back on the headboard. His eyes were closed but they snapped open when she entered the room.

They were grey. His eyes were the grey of a stormy sky, fringed with dark lashes, and they looked straight into hers as though he could see right into her soul.

"I've brought you some broth," she said, slightly breathless though she had no idea why.

"It smells wonderful," he said as she placed the tray on the small table beside her bed. His voice was smooth textured, sending a shiver right through her.

"I'll let you eat in peace," she told him, turning away.

"No! Wait," he said. "I'd really like it if you stayed and kept me company."

Chloe hesitated in the doorway. She really should check on her mother, but perhaps it wouldn't hurt if she stayed. Just for a little bit. Perching on the edge of the chair, she watched him take a few sips of broth and a bite of the bread before asking, "Where are you from?"

"I was born on —" he broke off what he was going to say and gave a rueful chuckle. "You know something? I never knew the name of the world I was born on. But my ancestors are from a world called Ardraci."

"Ardraci," she repeated, knowing her mother would wish every detail. "Have you ever been to this world of your ancestors?"

"Yes, briefly." A frowned flitted across his face. "But I did not feel comfortable there and so I left again. What about you? Are you alone here?"

"No, my mother is here as well, just down the hall. She worked in the mines, like me, until she became too sick to do so."

"I'm sorry," he said. And she could see that he meant what he said. "Is it serious?"

Chloe looked away from him and sighed. "Many of the miners suffer from the same illness, but most of them recover. My mother has been having a difficult time regaining her strength. The mine doctor comes to see her once a week, but . . ." She shrugged.

"Perhaps she just needs time," he suggested.

"Perhaps." Deliberately changing the subject, she asked, "Where were you going, before you crashed here?"

"I was on a scientific expedition, following an anomaly through space."

"Oh," she said in surprise. "You're a scientist." Somehow that just didn't seem to fit him. She saw him more as an adventurer.

"Not really," he said with his ready grin. "Just in this one case. And we've seen how that turned out."

They shared a laugh that died quickly as they stared at one another. To shake off the uncomfortable sensation, Chloe got up and picked up the tray. "You should rest now, Zephryn. Like my mother, you need to build up your strength."

"The broth was delicious Chloe, thank you."

"You're welcome," she said.

As she carried the tray out of the room she could feel his eyes on her. For no reason she could name, the feeling made her smile.

Chapter Three

Much to Zephryn's delight, the lovely Chloe came back after she disposed of the tray to see if there was anything else he needed.

Regretfully he shook his head. "I feel as though I have imposed on your hospitality long enough. I should be getting back to my ship to see what kind of damage was done to it."

"Really, you've been no trouble at all," she said rather quickly. "You should stay and rest, regain your strength before returning to your ship."

If he didn't know better, he'd think she almost looked frightened at the idea of him leaving. He couldn't shake the feeling there was something wrong here.

"I—"

There was a sudden pounding noise. Chloe jumped to her feet, face suddenly pale. "That's the door. I need to see who it is." She hesitated, then added. "Please, you need to stay here and not make any noise, no matter what you may hear. I'll explain when I return."

Without waiting for a reply she hurried from the room, closing the door firmly behind her. Zephryn stared at the closed door in bewilderment. Something was very wrong here.

Get dressed. Now. Da'nat's voice filled his mind.

"What? Why? What's going on?"

Quiet! Answer with your mind.

Zephryn caught the sense of urgency from the Ilezie. His feet hit the floor as he snagged his clothes from the chair. Quickly he began pulling them on.

All right, I'm getting dressed. Now tell me what's going on.

You must hide.

Hide? Zepheryn looked around the small room. *Where am I supposed to hide?*

Under the bed - hurry!

He could hear Chloe as she answered the door - she sounded angry. There were at least two other voices, both male. His first impulse was to go help her and he'd taken two steps towards the bedroom door when Da'nat's voice stopped him.

If they find you here it will be worse for her than for you. Hide. Now!

With a last glance towards the door, Zephryn finally dropped to the floor and wriggled under the bed. It was a tight fit, but he managed to work his way as close to the wall as he could.

I'm under the bed. Now will you tell me what's going on?

Quiet. And listen.

The voices outside grew louder, either drawing closer or raised in anger, he couldn't tell which. But he was able to make out what was being said.

"You have no right to just barge in here!" Chloe said.

"We have every right. This house is the property of the Mining Guild —" a male voice was saying.

"Which we pay rent for!"

"—and we're doing a search of all houses."

"Go ahead with your search," a second male ordered. "I need to have a word in private with Miss Chloe here."

"Get your hand off me!" There was the sound of the bedroom door opening. "How dare you! You have no right to invade my personal space!"

Zephryn heard the sound of footsteps and the door closing again. What by all the winds was going on here? As much as he wanted to find out, he realized Da'nat had been right to have him hide.

"I want you to tell me everything you know about the crash last night," the angry male demanded.

"What's to tell? A meteorite slipped through the protection grid and buried itself in the mountain. It happens all the time."

"That was no meteorite, and you know it."

"But what else could manage to slip through the protection grid?" Chloe asked.

"I think it was a ship, and I want you to find it for me."

"Me? You know I can't do anything like that Gannon."

Zephryn could hear movement in the room but could see nothing from where he lay. But he could certainly feel the slight tremor beneath him and he couldn't help but wonder how stable this area was.

"I think you can do a lot more than you let on," Gannon said, his voice suddenly calm.

"Th-that's crazy. You know I'm different from my mother. I don't have nearly her range of skills."

"If I ever find out you've been holding out on me . . ." He let the threat hang in the air.

"You know I would never do anything like that Gannon," Chloe said, a placating tone to her voice.

"Just remember, it's in your own best interest, and that of your mother, to make sure you use your talents for the benefit of the Mining Guild."

The tremor in the floor became more pronounced.

There was a sharp rap on the door.

"All clear," the first man's voice rang out.

"I'll be right there," Gannon yelled back. "Mark my words, I'm going to find that ship and whoever was flying it. I want you out there with the search crews tomorrow."

"But what about the new vein of ore? We're so close . . ."

"It can wait. I want that ship!"

* * * * *

Chloe rested her head against the closed door, breath coming out in a shuddering sigh. What had she been thinking? Hiding the ship, hiding the pilot in her own home . . . If Gannon ever found out she had anything to do with their disappearance, they were all dead. Or worse.

Many things had crashed on the surface before, and many of them Gannon had never found. But he'd never done a house to house search before. Not even after there'd been an escape from the mines.

It had been so close. And what happened to Zephryn?

Making sure the door was locked, she pushed away from it and headed back to her room.

"Zephryn?" she called out tentatively.

"Is it safe to come out?"

His voice was muffled and she looked around curiously, unable to pinpoint the source.

"Yes, they're gone. At least for now."

Her bed shifted slightly and she watched in shocked amusement as he began to wriggle his way out from under it. Halfway out he suddenly stopped.

"Damn it! I'm caught on something."

Chloe gave a strangled laugh. How had he ever managed to fit under there in the first place? "How did you know to hide?"

He gave a jerk, grunted, and the bed hopped in place. "Intuition." Another tug and he was free. "I believe this is yours." He rose to his feet, holding aloft an undergarment she'd lost weeks ago.

Face aflame, Chloe snatched it out of his hand.

"Now, I think we need to talk," he said.

"I—" The sound of a bell's chime cut her off. "That's my mother. I'll be right back."

Chloe hurried down the hall to her mother's room. Just her luck he wanted to talk. This just kept getting worse and worse. What was she supposed to tell him? She hoped her mother was lucid enough to tell her what to do.

Not only was Tierra awake, she was reasonably alert. "What by all the stars is going on, girl? Who was that man that invaded my bedroom?"

"Are you all right?" Chloe tried to straighten the blankets over her mother but her hand was slapped away.

"Stop fussing and answer me."

She sighed and sat on the edge of the bed. "Gannon's doing a house to house search for the pilot of the ship that crashed."

Tierra's eyes narrowed. "How does he know it was a ship?"

"I don't know, but he wants me out with the search crew tomorrow. Mother—"

"You hid the ship and brought the pilot here, like I told you?"

"Yes, but why—"

"I'd like to know why too," Zephryn said from the doorway.

Chloe gasped and turned so fast she nearly fell off the bed. "I told you I'd be right back!"

"I've never liked waiting," he said with a cheeky grin.

Tierra eyed him, a frown on her face. "You'd be Wind, from the looks of you."

"Yes ma'am. Zephryn WE-02-47-03, at your service." He gave a slight bow.

"Too bad," Tierra muttered. "We can't hide you in the cave."

"Why not?" Chloe asked, utterly confused by the turn the conversation had taken.

"Wind Elementals are notoriously claustrophobic. We'll have to see if Granny knows some place we can hide him."

"Wind Elemental?" Chloe looked from Zephryn to her mother. "What's a Wind Elemental?"

"Show her, boy."

Zephryn fixed his beautiful grey eyes on her. Suddenly, Chloe felt a breath of air, like a ghostly hand caressing her face. When the caress started to move downwards, she shook it off, jumping to her feet. "Stop it!"

"Sorry," he said, looking not one bit sorry at all. "And actually ma'am," he looked towards Tierra. "Caves don't bother me at all. I was pretty much raised in a cave."

"Excellent. Chloe can show—"

"Chloe isn't doing anything until you tell her what's going on!" She felt like stamping her foot, but didn't want to appear childish.

Zephryn's eyes narrowed as he looked from her to her mother and back again. "How did you know I was an Elemental?" he asked. Then his eyes widened. "I don't know why I didn't see it before. You're—" he broke off what he was going to say as Tierra shook her head slightly.

"Stop it! Both of you!" Chloe had had enough. She glared at the pair of them. "Nobody says another word unless it's to answer my questions."

Her mother was shocked into silence while Zephryn was back to looking amused.

"First of all, how did you know it was a ship that crashed?" she asked her mother.

"The earth told me." Though Tierra said it in a decisive tone, she plucked at the bed clothes and wouldn't look at Chloe.

Chloe's eyes narrowed. There was more to it than that, but for some reason her mother was being evasive. "All right. But why was it so important to hide the ship?"

"Use your head, girl. We wouldn't want Gannon to find the ship."

"But what difference would it have made to us? No offense," she added with a glance towards Zephryn.

"None taken. But I agree, what difference would it have made if anyone found my ship? Under the articles of space—"

Tierra made a rude noise. "You think Gannon cares anything for any law but his own? He would have confiscated your ship and you'd spend the rest of your life so deep in the mine you'd forget what the sun looked like."

"Surely—" Chloe began.

Her mother cut her off with a decisive gesture. "We need that ship more than Gannon does."

"Whatever for?"

"Why to escape, girl."

Chapter Four

Chloe felt a chill at her mother's words. Escape? There was only one escape from the mining colony for people like them, and she'd been on burial detail enough times to know it.

"Mother, what—" But it was too late. Tierra's eyes had closed again and Chloe knew they'd get nothing more from her until she'd rested. Not that what she'd said had made a great deal of sense in the first place.

"What's going on here?" Zephryn asked, all humour gone from his expression.

What indeed? Chloe rubbed her forehead. She could feel one of those severe headaches she'd been experiencing lately starting up.

"She won't awaken again until tomorrow," she said. "We can talk in the kitchen."

She led the way and once he was seated at the tiny wooden table tucked into the corner, she put the kettle on to boil, shaking the last of the medicinal tea she had into one heavy, ceramic mug, and regular tea into the other.

"I don't know where to start," she admitted, setting the mugs on the table and sliding into the seat opposite Zephryn.

"Why don't you start with Gannon?"

"Gannon is the . . . manager, I guess you could call him, of the Righteous Angels Mine." She wrapped her cold hands around the mug in front of her. "His is the largest territory on Belspar - nothing happens here without his knowledge, or permission."

"Except the occasional crash, it seems."

She glanced up to see a wry smile on his face. "Yes, except for that."

"Tell me, Chloe, have other ships crashed here before?"

The way he said her name sent a shiver through her, making it hard to focus on his question. A shaft of pain stabbed through her head and she winced, but it helped clear her thoughts. "Twice, in the last few years. One was a trading vessel, there were no survivors."

"And the other?" he prompted when she took her time answering.

"The other was a small colony ship. There were twenty-three survivors, all conscripted to the mines."

Zephryn sat back in his chair with an oath. "How's Gannon able to get away with it?"

She shrugged. "He's the manager."

"Dictator is more like it," he muttered. "How much danger am I putting you and your mother in by being here."

Again, Chloe hesitated. "The danger is greater for you, than for us." At least she hoped it was. The tea was doing nothing to halt the progression of the headache. It felt like a group of tiny miners had set up shop in her skull.

"What about my ship? Are you sure—"

"Positive," she said, a little sharper than she intended.

"There's no chance of anyone finding it."

He stared at her for a moment, but when he spoke his voice was gentle. "I'm keeping you from your rest - I think the rest of my questions can wait until tomorrow. Your mother mentioned a cave that would be safe for me to stay in?"

Chloe shook her head, the motion sending waves of pain streaking through her skull. "Not tonight. They won't be back tonight so you should be safe enough here. I can show you the cave tomorrow."

"Are you all right?"

Trying to muster up a smile, she said, "It's just a headache. I'll be fine." At least she hoped she would. They were getting worse, and if she was down in the mine when one hit it sometimes caused her to become distracted. And being distracted was dangerous for them all down there.

Pushing away from the table she stood up, braced for the fresh wave of pain. The mugs rattled on the table as a tremor went through the ground.

"You can have my bed again tonight," she told Zephryn. "I can share with my mother."

"I don't want to put you out." He rose to his feet as well.

"It's no trouble. In the cold weather my mother and I often share her bed." In the cold weather it was the only way to keep warm in this poorly insulated house.

"Then I'll say good night."

"Good night, Zephryn." She gathered up the mugs to take to the sink.

"And Chloe?" She turned to find him watching her with those beautiful grey eyes. "Pleasant dreams."

* * * * *

When Zephryn awoke in the morning, Chloe had already left to join the search party. His frustration level was on the rise, but no matter how badly he wanted answers to his ever-increasing number of questions, he couldn't bring himself to disturb Chloe's mother. It hadn't escaped his notice how thin and pale the woman was. There was no question she was seriously ill.

All this secrecy didn't sit well with him. He'd had enough of secrets growing up. It was too bad his friend Kairavini wasn't here. He'd always enjoyed a good secret.

He prowled through the small house, unable to stay still. There wasn't much to see. Besides the two bedrooms there was a kitchen with just enough space for a table and chairs. Along one wall was a tall cupboard, beside which was a sink, and along the opposite wall were more cupboards above and below a countertop that had a heating unit at one end and a cooling unit at the other. The lack of windows made it seem very utilitarian. The small sitting room at the front had a rocking chair and an overstuffed sofa, along with a long, low table in the center and a shelf holding an assortment of rocks.

Chloe had left clean towels in the bathroom and he helped himself to a shower. When he was finished, he opened the door to find a tiny, grey-haired woman with an extremely large weapon pointed at him. She was dressed in a long, faded grey skirt and a bright red blouse, with a white apron over top. Without being told to, he raised his hands.

"And who might you be?" the woman demanded.

Her voice was high and sharp, and he was hard pressed not

to smile. She was so tiny his wind could easily pick her right up and carry her away. "My name's Zephryn, ma'am."

"You'd be that pilot they're searching for, I'd guess."

"I guess so." There didn't seem to be any point in lying.

"Hmph!" The old woman tucked her weapon away in a pocket under her apron. "I might've guessed Chloe and her mother would be right in the thick of things. Have you had yer breakfast yet?"

"Ma'am?" Zephryn figured it was safe enough to lower his hands.

"Don't 'ma'am' me, son. The name's Granny." She turned and led the way to the kitchen.

Too bemused to do anything else, Zephryn followed in her wake and was told to park himself in one of the kitchen chairs. Granny was obviously familiar with the place because it wasn't long before he had a steaming plate in front of him.

"You don't talk much. I like that in a man."

He opened his mouth to speak and she waved a large spoon at him. "Eat first. Then you can ask questions."

Zephryn was starting to believe that he'd hit his head worse than he thought in the crash and was dreaming all this - Chloe, her mother, this whole thing. It was all just some pain induced hallucination. But he didn't believe hallucinations could cook this well. Breakfast was delicious and he quickly cleaned his plate.

"I like a man with an appetite too," Granny said. "My Wilmott had a good appetite, rest his soul. Now there was a man that was pleasure to cook for." She sat down in the chair opposite his, hands folded neatly on the table. "Fire away, son."

"I beg your pardon?"

She frowned. "I didn't take you for addled in the head. Your questions. Ask away. You must have a million of them."

"I don't know where to start."

Ask her if she knows how Chloe and her mother came to be on this world, Da'nat's voice whispered in his mind.

Zephryn gave a start. *Where have you been? Did you—*

Ask her.

Why?

They're Elementals. They should not be here.

Zephryn quickly pulled himself together as the old woman stared at him with fathomless eyes. "Do you know how Chloe and her mother ended up here?"

"What makes you think they're not here by choice?"

"It's just … they seem a little out of place. And the mother said something about needing my ship to escape. Escape from what?"

Granny sighed. "It seems like a lifetime ago. I guess for Chloe it was."

He waited patiently.

"Tierra was a stowaway on a freighter. Don't know what she was running from, but she was afraid for her life. And for the life of the child she was carrying. She was discovered just as the ship made port here. Primar, he was the mine master back then, he was all for making her the freighter's responsibility, but Tierra begged to talk to him. Don't know what all was said, but he paid the freighter's captain for her passage and she stayed here. Once she had her baby she worked in the mine to pay off the debt."

Zephryn frowned. "But wouldn't that debt have been paid off a long time ago?"

28

"Of course it was!"

"Then why are they still here?"

"My guess is Tierra made herself a little too useful. No way was Primar about to let her leave. He kept adding to her debt - medical bills for birthing Chloe, food, shelter . . ."

"But that's—"

"But that's what? Illegal?" Granny snorted. "Of course it is. This whole damn place is illegal. But who's going to do anything about it? Then Gannon took over and things just got worse."

"This Gannon . . . I don't understand why Chloe would bring me here if it's so dangerous for her and her mother."

"Tierra must have told her to. And she'd have her reasons, Tierra would."

"Just how sick is she?"

"Normally, the dust sickness passes in a matter of weeks. Tierra's been sick for years now."

"Chloe said you've been looking after her . . ."

"I do what I can, but Gannon insists on the mine doctor looking in on her once a week. I think, but I can't prove it, that the mine doctor gives her something that keeps her weak."

"Then why do you let her keep taking it?"

Granny's hands clenched into fists. "Do you think the likes of me is allowed in there during his visits? It's probably an injection of some kind to make sure whatever it is gets into her system. If it was pills we could get rid of them."

"That's criminal! There must be something you can do, someone you can go to . . ."

Granny looked at him bleakly. "He works for Gannon, and Gannon is the one in charge."

"So let me get this straight," Zephryn said slowly. "The doctor works for Gannon, not the people he's supposed to be caring for. And he's been giving something to Chloe's mother to keep her sick so that Gannon can force Chloe to work off the cost of the medical bills by working in the mines."

"That about sums it up son."

Chapter Five

Granny went to check on Tierra leaving Zephryn alone in the kitchen. The moment she was out of sight he focused his mind.

Da'nat?

There was no response.

Damn it, Da'nat! I know you were listening in. Talk to me!

What would you have me say?

Zephryn pushed back from the table and began to pace in the tiny space. *For starters, where are you?*

I'm aboard the ship of course.

Fine. Tell me where the ship is and I'll join you. We need to get out of this place and go tell the authorities what's going on.

You make it sound very simple. Trust me when I say it is not.

Then what do we do? Zephryn stopped pacing.

We have patience.

He blew out an exasperated breath. Trust an Ilezie to come up with such an answer. Before he was able to start an argument he had no chance of winning, Granny was back.

"She wants to see you, sonny."

"Who does?" he asked in surprise.

Granny rolled her eyes. "Tierra, of course. Who else do you think's in here?"

Feeling just slightly dull-witted, he followed her back to Tierra's bedroom.

Chloe's mother was sitting up in bed, eyes clear but cheeks flushed. Zephryn shot a glance towards Granny who shook her head.

"I need you to make me a promise," Tierra said without preamble.

"Are you sure you should be—"

She waved off his concern. "I'm fine at the moment."

"Then maybe we should wait for Chloe." Zephryn had a feeling that whatever Tierra was about to say was going to complicate things. And the last thing he needed right now was another complication.

"No. I want you to promise that if anything happens to me, you'll see that Chloe's taken care of."

"But—"

"Promise me!"

"All right! I promise." The last thing he wanted to do was to upset Tierra and make her sicker. She looked like she was barely holding on as it was.

"Good." Tierra settled back against the pillows again. "Now there's a couple of things you need to know about Chloe. First of all, she doesn't know she's an Elemental."

"I knew you were Elementals! Wait. How can she not know?"

"Don't mistake me. She knows she's got the earth gift, just not what it means."

"But . . . why didn't you just explain it to her?" Wouldn't she have had questions when she passed through her *tespiro*? How hard would it have been to tell her where she was from and what her people could do?

"Chloe is special. She has more gift in her little finger than I do in my whole body," Tierra continued as though he hadn't spoken. "If Gannon realized half of what she could do . . ."

"She's been slipping," Granny put in.

"How do you mean?" Tierra asked sharply.

Zephryn was curious about that himself.

"Haven't you felt it? The tremors in the earth? She's lucky she hasn't caused an accident."

"I noticed, twice since I've been here," Zephryn said. "Once when that Gannon confronted her and then again when we were talking in the kitchen. She said she had a headache."

"Headaches?" Tierra looked troubled. "She never said anything to me about any headaches."

"I'm sorry. I didn't—" Zephryn stopped. A headache in itself wasn't necessarily dangerous, but it might be the sign of Chloe having difficulty controlling her power. There was no way he could have known it was a secret, but Zephryn felt like smacking himself in the head anyway.

"She just didn't want to worry you is all," Granny interrupted. "They're nothing my special tea can't handle."

Tierra shifted in the bed. "I think I could use a cup of one of your teas right now."

"Hmph!" Granny sniffed. "If you wanted me to leave, you just had to say so."

It was obvious, the effort Tierra was making to calm herself. "I'm sorry, but I need to have a word in private with our guest here."

"Fine. But don't tire yourself out too much." Muttering under her breath, Granny left for the kitchen.

"Where is he?" Tierra asked as soon as the old woman was out of ear shot.

"Where's who?"

"The Ilezie. I know he was on the ship with you."

"I—I—" For the second time, shock rendered him speechless.

You may tell her, Da'nat said in his mind.

"He's still on the ship."

"I need to speak with him. In person."

"I don't—"

Tell her I will be with her when she next awakens.

You will?

Yes.

Zephryn had reached his limit of surprises. If he received one more, he just might snap.

* * * * *

Rock grated against rock as the earth shifted minutely. Chloe stepped back as loose dirt rained down and quickly refocused her attention on the scanner she held. She'd been thinking about Zephryn again and became distracted. At this rate she was going to cause a cave-in. She needed to be more careful.

"You sure you know what you're doing? This section looks like it was mined out years ago."

The man who spoke was new to the mine, and could therefore be forgiven his ignorance.

"Mind your manners," Martin, the crew chief said. "Chloe's

the best damn Seeker on the planet. We're lucky to have her on our team."

Seekers were the ones who told the mining crews where to dig. Though they were equipped with scanners, most had an uncanny sense of where the best ores and minerals were to be found. Chloe's scanner was just for show, but only she and Gannon knew that.

"This is taking way too long. I'm telling you, she's taking us in the wrong direction. There's nothing down here!"

It was the same thing every time someone new joined the crew. They all thought she was too young, too small, or too pretty to know what she was doing. This one, she couldn't even remember his name, had been complaining since they started this morning. She'd had enough of it, and could tell the rest of the crew had too. Time to teach this guy a lesson.

She turned suddenly. "You think you can do better? Be my guest." She thrust the scanner towards him.

His mouth opened and closed several times before an angry expression filled his face and he took it from her. "Fine by me. I certainly can't do a worse job than you."

Chloe stepped back and waved him forward. He went ahead, holding the scanner like a talisman. Silently, she motioned to the rest of the crew to don their masks. Martin caught on to what was about to happen and grinned.

This section of the mine was riddled with gas pockets that sent false readings to the scanners. It took an experienced Seeker to avoid them, which was why Chloe's crew was here and not another. The gas behind the rock at this point was not dangerous in itself, but it was extremely malodorous.

With a cry of triumph, the man struck at the rock and then reeled back, coughing and choking as gas hissed out of the small crack he'd made. Tears streaming from his eyes, he glared at the rest of the crew, who were roaring with laughter.

"This is your fault!" He took a step towards Chloe, brandishing the scanner. "You did that on purpose!"

"Me? But I don't know what I'm doing." She couldn't help the mocking tone to her voice. "How would I be able to tell the difference between a gas pocket and a vein of aphalite?"

He took a swing at her with the scanner but was intercepted by Martin. "You're off the crew," Martin said, all humour gone from his face. He pried the scanner from the man's hand.

"What? You can't do that! Gannon himself—"

"Then you can explain to Gannon himself how you went after one of his Seekers." Martin was implacable. The rest of the crew had become silent.

The man glared at Chloe. "You'll pay for this." His glare swept over the rest of the crew. "Mark my words, you'll all pay for this!"

He spun on his heel and stalked off through the passage.

"You all right?" Martin's voice gentled as he handed Chloe back the scanner.

Chloe nodded. "It was just a joke," she said in a small voice. "I didn't mean—"

"Stop. He had it coming to him. You saved me the trouble of dumping him down one of the shafts. Accidentally of course." He grinned at her.

She mustered up an answering smile. "Whatever you say, chief."

It would be so much easier if she could work without a crew. Not only could she find the minerals they sought quicker, she could extract them by herself as well. Although if Gannon ever found out she could do more than just locate specific metals and minerals in the earth . . . she shuddered just to think about it.

The tunnel branched out ahead and they came to a stop. "Which way, Chloe?"

Catching her bottom lip between her teeth, she made a show of pointing the scanner in both directions. Reaching out with her gift, she was able to detect the mineral they were seeking.

"Either will give us what we want," she said finally. "We'll need to call in extra crews. This vein is huge."

There were cheers from the men around her. A vein large enough to warrant extra crews meant bonuses for the ones who found it.

"Just let me collect a few samples and then we're done for the day," Martin said.

Chloe nodded wearily. She'd been up at first light to join the search party looking for Zephryn's ship, and put in a full day here. It was more than time to call it a day. And hopefully finding an aphalite deposit of this size would improve Gannon's mood.

He'd been incensed when they found no trace of the ship he was sure had crashed. No matter how far they looked there was no trace of a crash, which further angered him. Chloe's heart had been in her mouth and she couldn't prevent the small earth tremors that escaped her control as they passed over the site where the ship was buried. But Zephryn's ship must have been made of some kind of reflective alloy because nothing showed up on Gannon's scanner.

Martin sent the brilliant blue samples on ahead and the rest of the crew trudged along behind him as their shift ended. One of the support staff was there to meet them as they emerged from the mine.

"Chloe? Gannon would like to see you in his office."

Chapter Six

Zephryn had not realized how much he'd become used to being able to come and go as he pleased until he was no longer able to do so. When Granny left she warned him to stay away from the door and windows, not that he'd needed the reminder. The last thing he wanted to do was cause trouble for Chloe and her mother. Tierra was sleeping again, which left pacing and thinking as the only way to occupy his time.

What did Tierra mean when she said Chloe didn't know she was an Elemental? Obviously Chloe used her gift in her work, so she had to know she was different from everyone else. Clearly Granny was keeping their secret. He wondered who else knew about Chloe's gift?

Wait. Tierra said something about how Gannon didn't know the true extent of Chloe's power . . . just how powerful was she? And if she was so powerful, why were they still here?

"Your thoughts chase each other like leaves in a whirlpool."

Zephryn yelped and spun around. "Da'nat! But where—" The diminutive creature stood right behind him, his form covered in a shapeless brown robe.

"Take me to the woman who would demand the appearance of the Ilezie." For such a tiny being, Da'nat's presence filled the room, and when he used that voice of command there was nothing to do but obey.

Pushing his own questions aside, Zephryn led the way down the hall. He knocked gently on the door to Tierra's room before pushing it open. She was awake and waiting.

"Leave us," Da'nat ordered.

A small gust of wind swirled through the room as Zephryn's frustration got the better of him.

"We will talk later," Da'nat said, in a gentler tone of voice.

With a sigh Zephryn left, closing the door gently behind him. He only went as far as the kitchen, where he could keep an eye on the door, and resumed his pacing. It was almost enough to make him wish to be back in Dr. Uri Arjun's compound, where all he had to worry about was his next breeding. Almost.

He had no idea how long Da'nat and Tierra talked, but it felt like forever before the door opened. Zephryn took one look at Da'nat's face and stemmed the tide of questions about to spill forth. Instead he asked only one.

"What did she say to you?" His voice was hushed.

Da'nat looked at him silently. Where before his presence seemed overwhelming, now he seemed . . . diminished.

The door at the front of the house rattled and Zephryn glanced down the hallway. "That must be Chloe. Why don't you sit down and gather your thoughts while I—" He looked back down but the Ilezie was gone.

"Da'nat?" He turned in a full circle but there was no trace of him.

Da'nat? Where'd you go? Are you all right?

No.

No? No what?

Later.

Zephryn was ready to scream with frustration, but then Chloe was standing in the doorway of the kitchen, looking as worn out as he felt, and all he could think about was taking care of her.

"You must be starving," she said. "Just give me a minute to get cleaned up and—"

He was already shaking his head. "Not a chance."

It only took two long steps to bring him to her and when she looked up at him in surprise he had to resist the urge to kiss her. Instead he took her by the shoulders and turned her gently around.

"Go ahead and get cleaned up, take a nice relaxing bath if you like, I'll fix us something to eat."

"You will?"

He chuckled at the doubt in her voice. "Yes, I will."

She took a step down the hall and stopped. "But my mother . . ."

"Your mother is sleeping." He didn't know how he knew this, he just did. "And I'll make enough for her too. It can be heated up when she awakens."

"A bath would be nice," she murmured.

"Go!" he ordered.

As she continued on to the bathroom he turned to the kitchen cupboards. Surely he could come up with something to dazzle her with. He did not stop to wonder why he felt it was important he do so.

* * * * *

Chloe eased into the warm water filling the tub with a sigh. Normally if she was feeling stressed she'd stop for a soak in the hot spring on her way home from the mine, but after her encounter with Gannon all she'd wanted to do was go home.

While she hadn't been surprised at being called into his office at the end of her shift, she was surprised that the new recruit wasn't there as well. She was feeling just a hint of guilt over the prank she'd played on him. It had been an irresponsible thing to do, but her temper had been getting the best of her lately.

But there was no sign of the new recruit, just Gannon waiting for her over by the round table he usually had his paperwork spread out on. There was chilled wine and selection of food waiting for her as well; the wine wasn't the only thing feeling a chill as she'd stepped over his threshold.

"I thought a little celebration might be in order," Gannon told her, popping the cork to the bottle.

"Celebration?"

"Of your most recent find. Martin says that vein of aphalite will need a double crew to work it."

He brought her a glass of wine and she had no choice but to take it. Other veins had been just as rich, if not richer. There was something else going on.

There was a light in his eye that she'd seen once or twice before and things started to click into place. She was tired enough that the tremors escaped before she could stop them.

Gannon frowned and went over to the computer. "We've been having more of these lately, but we're having problems locking down the epicentre. It keeps moving."

"That's very unusual."

He glanced up at her. "You wouldn't know anything about this, would you?"

"Me? I work with the ore, not in seismology."

"This tremor was almost right under us." He looked back down at the computer. "It's almost as if . . ."

Chloe's eyes went brown. Another, stronger tremor, registered several miles from the mine.

"Thank you for the wine," she said, setting down her untouched glass. "I really need to go check on my mother." Then she'd fled before he could stop her.

She wasn't naive, she knew Gannon wanted her, and for more than just her work in the mine. He'd been keeping his distance these last few years though, as if some invisible line had been drawn. But now it looked like he was ready to cross that line and she had no idea what to do about it.

The water in the tub began to tremble and she tried to calm herself again. She needed to forget about Gannon and the mine for now. For tonight at any rate. Instead she would focus on the man in her kitchen, making her dinner.

Granny always told her that things happened for a reason. So there had to be a reason that Zephryn's ship crashed on this world, out of all the habitable worlds in the Deadlands. The problem was he seemed to be filled with as many questions as she was.

Chloe wasn't stupid. She knew her mother was worried about something, hiding something from her. And it was something pretty important, she'd bet her life on it. Granny was probably in on it too. She was more than just the local healer, she really was like a grandmother to them.

They thought they were sheltering her, keeping their secrets. But she also knew there was more going on with Tierra's illness than they were letting on. She always seemed worse after Gannon's doctor visited, but when she'd confronted Gannon about it he'd adopted a wounded expression and claimed to be hurt that she could even think he'd want to keep Tierra ill. Why, together Chloe and Tierra could make the Righteous Angels mine the richest in all the Deadlands.

And now here was Zephryn, and her mother seemed to want to draw him into whatever was going on as well. Which was obviously more than just her illness. But what? And why did she get the feeling Zephryn knew something she didn't?

Her mother had called him a Wind Elemental, and she'd felt the touch of the wind on her face, like a caress . . . But what exactly was a Wind Elemental, and what did it have to do with them escaping?

Chloe sat up straight suddenly, water sloshing in the tub. It had to have something to do with their ability to sense and manipulate the earth.

There was only one way to get some answers she decided, reluctantly leaving the tub. She and Zephryn needed to talk.

Chapter Seven

Zephryn tried contacting Da'nat mentally a few times but was met with silence. To see the Ilezie shaken like that was a little unnerving. There was something going on here that was much more than simply crashing on a mining planet. The niggling feeling they were here for some other reason was just too strong to ignore. But what other reason could there be?

He had just gathered the ingredients for dinner when he heard Tierra's bell. He glanced down the hall towards the bathroom but there was no sign of Chloe. With a resigned sigh, he wiped his hands off on a cloth and went over to knock softly on the door before opening it.

Tierra was looking more rested than he'd seen her thus far and she smiled when she saw him. "I thank you most kindly for bringing the Ilezie to me."

He snorted. "I didn't bring him anywhere. Da'nat comes and goes as he pleases."

"It has ever been so with the Ilezie." She nodded. "Tell me, young man. Is it true that Dr. Arjun is no more?"

Her question caught him by surprise. "You knew Arjun?"

The very name had become somewhat of a curse on Ardraci.

"Oh, yes." There was a bitter edge to her voice. "He's the reason we've been hidden here all these years."

"You escaped from the Program," he guessed.

Tierra began to cough and he realized she was not as well as she appeared.

"As much as I would enjoy hearing your story, I think you need to rest. Why don't I finish making diner and we can talk afterwards?"

"Yes, I think you are right." Her eyelids began to droop. "Chloe needs to hear this too."

Zephryn left her dozing and finished making dinner, thoughts swirling through his head. So, Chloe and her mother had been part of the same program that created him. That would account for the strength of Chloe's gift. But they must have escaped when she was quite young, unless Chloe was just very good at covering up what she knew.

He was so immersed in his thoughts that he didn't even notice Chloe hovering in the doorway to the kitchen.

"Something smells good."

The spoon he was holding clattered to the countertop. Zephryn pressed a hand to his chest in mock fright "I'll need to get you a bell. You just about gave me a heart attack."

She smiled at his antics and he felt a zing somewhere in the region of his heart. "You look beautiful." The words escaped before he could stop them, but he wasn't about to take them back. She really did look beautiful. Her auburn hair was unbound and tumbled past her shoulders, and she was dressed in a flowing tunic and pants of dark green that had a hint of shine to it.

Zephryn pulled out a chair. "Allow me," he said with a flourish.

Blushing faintly, Chloe took her seat. He put a steaming plate in front of her before taking his own seat. "I've already taken a plate to your mother. She seems to be doing a little better and wants to talk to us after we finish."

"She always seems to rally, right before the mine doctor comes to visit."

He wondered that she didn't seem to make the connection between the doctor's visit and the worsening of her mother's condition, but decided against questioning her about it. He didn't want to make her feel bad if she hadn't noticed. Lapsing into silence again, they concentrated on their food.

"I never gave food preparation much thought when I was growing up," Zephryn said to break the silence between them before it became too great. "I just ate what was put in front of me."

"I'm sure that's the way it is with most children." Chloe kept her eyes on her plate. "I was the same until mother started getting sick, and then I decided I wanted to learn to cook to help ease her burden."

"I never knew my mother."

At those softly spoke words she looked up at him. "Pardon me?"

He gave her a flash of a smile. "I never knew my mother, I grew up in a compound where our food came from dispensers. Most of the time it was pretty bland."

"You were raised in a compound?"

"It wasn't so bad. We were well taken care of." Interesting, she didn't appear to know about Arjun's compound after all. Maybe Tierra escaped when the compound was moved. But no, that didn't seem right either. He'd put Chloe's age as around the same as his and the compound was moved when he was ten. She would have to have been a baby when Tierra escaped, otherwise they would not have been together.

"Where did you learn to cook then?"

The question was not the one he was anticipating and it made him smile. "While I was in the compound I did a study on cooking, even though I lacked the equipment to do any practical work. But when I went to Ardraci I was able to hone my skills."

"You are very skillful indeed," Chloe said, smiling back. "This was wonderful. Thank you."

"Why don't we leave these dishes to soak while we talk with your mother? We don't want to tire her out too much just when she's feeling better."

At that a troubled look passed over Chloe's face, though she nodded in agreement. "I'm afraid even on her good days it doesn't take much to tire her. But if she wants to talk, then it must be something important."

Zephryn felt a wave of sympathy. She had no idea.

* * * * *

Chloe didn't know what possessed her to dress up after her bath; she refused to admit that she'd done it for Zephryn. After all, he was a stranger, and a transient one at that. As soon as it was safe she'd unbury his ship and he'd be gone. At least that's what she assumed would happen.

She felt awkward and tongue-tied around him; her skin felt

too tight. Talking with him while they ate put her more at ease, but she tensed up again as they entered her mother's room.

"Chloe, girl, you've often asked about your father and why he isn't with us, and the time has come for you to learn the truth."

Zephryn paused in the act of sitting down. "This sounds like something between mother and daughter, perhaps I should—"

"No." Tierra waved a hand at him. "Sit. You need to hear this too."

He sat on the chair and Chloe sat on the bed.

"We came from a world called Ardraci—" her words were cut off by a fit of coughing.

"Ardraci …" Chloe sounded the word out while her mother recovered. Where had she heard that word before? Suddenly, it came to her. "You said Ardraci was the planet you came from as well, didn't you?" she asked Zephryn.

He nodded. "It's where my people came from originally, yes."

"Mother, perhaps this should wait until you're stronger." She leaned forward and poured her mother a glass of water from the pitcher on the bedside table.

"No." Tierra took a sip and a couple of deep breaths. "Things have been set in motion . . . I need to tell you things." A couple more breaths and she was able to continue.

"When I was young and foolish, I became involved with a group that followed the teachings of Dr. Uri Arjun, an Ardraci scientist who sought to create the perfect elemental."

"Elemental." Chloe frowned. "You mentioned that before. And you," she turned to look at Zephryn, "She called you a Wind Elemental. But what exactly is an elemental?"

49

"There are four elements," Zephryn told her. "Wind, fire, water, and earth. An Elemental has a certain amount of control over one of these elements."

She was quick to put things together. "So because mother and I are able to sense things about the earth and manipulate it, that makes us Earth Elementals?" She turned back to her mother. "Are there others like us?"

"Yes," Tierra said. "Many others. Now let me finish."

Chloe made a concentrated effort to rein in her curiosity.

"Dr. Arjun's specialty was genetics, and he began experimenting with the Ardraci genome to try and isolate the factors that went into the elemental gifts. He preached about the purity of the Ardraci race and drew many idealistic young people to his side."

"And you were one of these followers?" Chloe guessed. "Is that how you met my father?"

"Quiet. And yes, it was through Arjun I met your father, so to speak." Tierra paused for another sip of water. "Arjun's followers provided him with financial support and aided him in his experiments. Later, they became test subjects as well."

"Test subjects!" Chloe shot a glance at Zephryn, who wouldn't meet her eyes.

"When Arjun began experimenting on human subjects, the Ardraci government tried to shut him down and we were forced to flee the planet."

"We? Of course, you were part of the group." Chloe felt a knot growing in her stomach. "What part did you play in this group of his?"

"A first I was just a technician, a medical assistant of sorts.

But we lost two of our ships when we escaped Ardraci, and we needed a wider gene pool than the one we brought with us, so Arjun had everyone tested - he'd invented some kind of device that was able to measure the strength of their elemental gift."

"And when he saw the strength of your gift?"

Tierra nodded. "He had me transferred from the lab to the breeding program."

"Where you were bred to my father." Chloe said, voice a mere whisper. "Were you at least willing?"

"I . . . I was not unwilling. But it was not the romantic encounter I had dreamed of. Afterwards I realized that there would be many more such encounters, should I stay with the program, and I decided to leave."

"I doubt it was that easy." Zephryn shifted in his seat, frowning.

"No, it most certainly was not," Tierra said with a rueful smile. "But I had a friend, Wynne Ignitus - she was a newly certified midwife and new to the program as well. With her help I was able to use an escape pod to flee the ship."

"Wait." Zephryn leaned forward. "That can't be right. Uri Arjun left Ardraci more than fifty years ago."

"Then how —" Chloe began.

"It was a stasis pod." He cut her off, the sudden realization stripping him of his manners. "You escaped in a stasis pod."

Tiera nodded. "Exactly so."

"What's a stasis pod?" Chloe asked.

"The big colony ships use them," Zephryn explained. "In fact, most colonists travel in stasis pods that can be ejected if anything happens to the ship. They're just big enough for a single person. Once you're inside it releases a preservation gas that suspends all life functions. They take minimal energy to maintain and they're fitted with a distress beacon. It's a really efficient system."

"We disabled the distress beacon so they wouldn't know when or where I'd left the ship. I was eventually found by a luxury liner, who revived me and set me down at their next port of call. I was too afraid to talk to the port authorities - Ardraci was not part of any of the planetary leagues when I left, and I wasn't sure what my reception would be if I was returned there. So I stowed away on a freighter that brought me here."

"But . . ." Zephryn stopped what he was about to say.

"But what?" Chloe prompted.

"How long were you in stasis?"

"Thirty-seven years." Before Chloe could ask why that was significant, Tierra told her. "It's not recommended that stasis be used for more than ten years at a time - twenty, at most. And no," she said to Zephryn. "I didn't know I was pregnant at the time."

Chapter Eight

Zephryn glanced at Chloe. She didn't appear to realize the significance of her what her mother just said.

"What? Why are you looking at me like that?"

He shifted his look towards Tierra, who avoided his eyes, and then back to Chloe. "Stasis pods were still a relatively new concept when your mother made use of one. In those early days it was chancy enough to use one for an extended period of time, but they were never used by immature beings or beings that were carrying offspring."

"Why not?" Though Chloe directed the question at him, her eyes were on her mother.

"Tests showed. . ." He couldn't bring himself to finish.

"Tests showed that significant genetic abnormalities could result," Tierra said. "But I didn't know I was carrying you at the time."

"And if you had?"

Tierra's face hardened. "It wouldn't have mattered. I'd have still taken the chance."

Chloe's eyes were huge in a face gone pale and Zephryn

wished there was something he could say or do that would make things better for her. The ground started to shake beneath them.

"Stop that!" Tierra snapped.

The shaking stopped, but Chloe looked close to tears.

"As soon as I found out I was pregnant I had them run a genetic scan. There's nothing wrong with you!"

"Except I'm a freak, like you!" Chloe rose from her seat and started pacing.

"You're not a freak!" Zephryn protested.

"Tell her," Tierra begged. "Tell her what would have happened if I'd stayed, what it was like growing up with Arjun."

Zephryn reached up and stopped Chloe as she paced, taking her by the hand and pulling her down into the chair next to his.

"If you're a freak, then I'm a bigger freak because I'm a second generation product of Arjun's program."

She looked like she wanted to believe him. Encouraged by the fact she didn't pull her hand back, he continued.

"Here's what your life would have been like had your mother stayed and you'd been born into the Program. At age two you would have been taken from your mother and put in a nursery with the other children born in the same year. At age five you're sent to the dormitories, one for girls and one for boys, but you'll stay with your year group until after you've reached *tespiro*."

"*Tespiro*, what's that?"

Zephryn shot a look towards Tierra who shook her head minutely.

"It's . . . a rite of passage where your elemental gift manifests itself."

"Oh." Chloe nodded. "It must happen early on then. I can't

remember a time when I wasn't able to use my gift."

His mouth opened, and shut again. She must be mistaken. Taking a deep breath, he continued. "You're given enough instruction to control your gift, to prevent accidents, but for the most part you won't need to worry about it because you'll have an inhibitor implanted in you so that you'll never know just how strong your gift is." Like his friend Ravi, the most power Water Elemental ever born, who grew up believing his gift was one of the weakest.

"The education you receive will be heavy on the sciences, and although you're encouraged to study whatever you wish independently, your activities will be monitored. You'll also receive instruction on procreation - that's the whole point of you being there, after all - but it's procreation in the most clinical way possible."

Chloe looked like she wanted to ask a question but didn't quite know how.

"Sex without emotion, girl," her mother said.

"Oh." A flush suffused her face and she snatched her hand back from his.

Zephryn stifled a grin.

"When you reach the proper age - eighteen for girls, nineteen for boys - you'll become part of the breeding program. You and a carefully selected Seeder will be taken to one of the breeding rooms where you'll . . . breed."

"What . . . what happens if the . . . breeding is unsuccessful?"

"You and the Seeder will be brought together once a day for five successive days and if, at the end of that time, pregnancy does not result, you'll be paired with a new Seeder the following month."

"I could not face such a life," Tierra said. "Nor would I have wished such a life on any of my offspring."

"The worst part is," Zephryn said quietly, "You would grow up thinking this life was normal. All forms of emotional attachment were discouraged, so you would have few, if any, friends. You would have no say in who were bred to, and no contact with any of your offspring after they were sent to the nursery. You would never know there was a world outside of the compound."

"It sounds so lonely."

"It was."

* * * * *

Chloe tried to imagine Zephryn's life, being raised in the compound. To grow up without knowing the love of a parent, to be discouraged from having friends . . . it didn't bear thinking of. There was a part of her that wanted to hurl herself into his arms to comfort him. Instead she got up and went over to her mother's bed, where she sat down beside her.

"I'm sorry I was so harsh with you." She looked over at Zephryn. "And I'm sorry for everything you went through as a child. How did you escape?"

"That's a story for another time, I think. Your mother appears to have worn herself out."

She looked down and found he was right. Tierra was fighting to keep her eyes open. "Rest now, mother." She leaned down and kissed her on the forehead.

"Change . . . it's coming." Tierra's eyes were closed and her breathing ragged. "No stopping it . . . should have prepared you for it . . ."

"Mother?" Chloe felt a stab of fear and glanced up at Zephryn. He got up and came over to stand beside her.

"Tierra?"

Her eyes snapped open suddenly and she pinned him with a look. "You have to help her; help them. You're the only one who can!"

"Help who with what?"

But it was too late. Her eyes were already closed again and Chloe could tell just by looking at her she wasn't going to waken again until morning. At Zephryn's questioning glance she shook her head and then led him out of the room. He followed her to the front room and sat down beside her on the sofa.

"Zephryn, have you any idea what she was talking about? The changes and . . . the rest?" She could only assume she was the one her mother wanted Zephryn to help, but help how, and with what? Could her mother have found out about Gannon bothering her?

He shook his head. "It didn't really make sense, almost as if . . ."

"Almost as if what?"

"Some of the Ardraci I met have visions of the future. Has your mother ever spoken like this before?"

Chloe took a moment to think about it. "Not really, no. Sometimes she'd say things I wouldn't understand, but I'd always assumed it was just fever talk."

Something flickered across his face, some emotion she didn't quite catch. She put a hand on his arm. "What is it?"

"I have a friend whose sister had visions . . ." His voice drifted off and he seemed to lose himself in a memory.

"And?"

Giving himself a slight shake he looked down at her, covering her hand with his. "Her visions needed interpretation and often left her weak. I just wondered if that might be part of why your mother is having trouble recovering from her illness."

It made a strange kind of sense, but if that were the case, why didn't her mother say something sooner? Chloe sighed.

"This is all so confusing."

Zephryn's hand tightened briefly on hers. "It's confusing for me as well."

"This friend of yours, did his sister have visions often?"

"I'm sorry, I don't know much more than I told you. We had a difficult time maintaining our friendship after we reached breeding age, and his sister died during the escape. He doesn't talk about her much - it's still too painful."

"How old were you when you escaped from the compound?"

"It's been a few months now, and I have to say that freedom takes some getting used to."

Chloe sat up straight so she could face him. "You've only been free for a few months? How were you able to stand it?"

"Many spent their entire lives there," he said quietly.

She couldn't help the tears that spilled down her cheeks. Zephryn pulled her into his arms, cradling her head on his shoulder. He felt so warm and alive; she couldn't imagine his cold, unfeeling childhood. Freedom wasn't something a person should have to get used to.

"It's all right," he said, running a soothing hand up and down her back. "Dr. Arjun's gone now and those of us who were raised in the compound have been reintegrated into Ardraci society."

Chloe sniffled, tears lessening. "I thought you said you didn't like Ardraci and you left."

He smiled. "I didn't feel useful there. I was offered the chance to be on a ship with several other Ardraci and I was happy to accept. I knew the rudiments of flight from my studies, so it didn't take me long to become a pilot."

"Like your cooking." Chloe raised her head.

"Exactly."

They stared at each other for the space of a few heartbeats. He reached out and gently brushed her tears away. Chloe shivered at his touch, held captive by his gaze. Slowly his head lowered and her eyes fluttered shut as their lips met.

Chapter Nine

Stop that, at once!

Da'nat's voice was like a bucket of cold water. Zephryn broke off the kiss but held Chloe close so she wouldn't think it was anything she'd done.

Get out of my head!

We need to talk.

Now you want to talk? In case you haven't noticed, this isn't a good time.

Chloe shifted in his arms, resting her head on his shoulder. He glanced down and gave a resigned sigh. Her eyes were closed, and it was no wonder, she was probably exhausted from her long day.

Fine. What is it that's so urgent?

There are things you need to know should you decide to continue.

Continue? Continue what? He glanced down at Chloe again and flushed. *Oh.*

Indeed.

Well I won't be continuing anything for a while, so what's so important that you couldn't wait to tell me?

The voice in his head went silent. A breeze swept through the room, echoing Zephryn's frustration.

Control yourself.

No, you talk to me! You tell me what's going on, what we're doing here!

You know as well as I. The anomaly we were following—

That's only part of the truth and you know it!

Inadvertently his grip on Chloe tightened and she murmured in her sleep. Gentling his hold again he waited until her breathing evened out before continuing the conversation in his mind.

We may have been attacked by the anomaly, but with our shields at full power we should have skimmed right over the security web. Something let us through. Someone wanted us here and I want to know who.

There was a moment of silence in his mind, then, *What do you recall of your instruction in tespiro?*

What? Zephryn was sure he hadn't heard the question right. *What has that got to do with why we're here?*

Humour me, Da'nat said.

All right, Zephryn said, hoping that if he answered Da'nat's question, Da'nat would answer his. *It's the transition where we come into our full elemental power. The stronger your gift, the worse the tespiro.*

And leading up to it?

Is the most dangerous time for an Ardraci. The elemental power builds until it's released all at once, triggering the transition. It . . . Again a breeze swept through the room and his eyes widened at a sudden thought.

Chloe didn't seem to know about tespiro. But with a gift as powerful as hers, how could she have undergone tespiro and not know it?

She could not.

But that would mean . . .

I do not believe she has undergone the transition.

Zephryn stared down at the woman sleeping in his arms. *But . . . is that even possible? Her gift is so strong, and she's been using it for years.*

I have never before heard of such a thing.

But . . . Zephryn thought back to all the warnings they were given of the hazards of *tespiro*, of elements out of control, of those in his year-group who were unprepared and returned to their element. *If she goes through her tespiro after using her element for so long, won't that be dangerous?*

Yes.

But if she tries to suppress it . . .

It would be even worse.

The headaches and earth tremors . . .

They may very well be early signs of the approach of tespiro.

Zephryn felt a chill go up his spine. *Is that what her mother meant when she asked that I help her? "Changes are coming," she said. She thinks I can help Chloe through her tespiro.*

Indeed.

Is she the one who opened the security net for us?

There was a distinct pause before Da'nat answered. *I do not believe so.*

* * * * *

When Chloe awoke, she was surprised to find herself in her own bed. Zephryn must have carried her to her room after she fell asleep.

Oh!

She sat up quickly, face heating. Not only did she fall asleep, she fell asleep while they were kissing! What must he think of her? Her first impulse was to lay back down and pull the covers over her head. How was she ever going to face him again?

Practicality finally won out. Much as she'd like to, she couldn't stay in bed forever. For one thing, she was starving, and she needed to check on her mother. As she got out of bed she caught sight of herself in the mirror above her dresser and grimaced. What had she been thinking, dressing up like this?

The green spider-silk pantsuit went back into the closet and she pulled out a pair of more casual draw-string pants and well-worn tunic instead. Hair up or down? When she was working she usually wore it pulled back off her face, but because she had the day off she decided to leave it down.

Finally running out of excuses, Chloe took a deep breath and left her bedroom. To her surprise, the kitchen was empty. She checked the bathroom but the door was open and there was no one inside. Zephryn wouldn't have been foolish enough to leave the house in broad daylight, would he?

Continuing down the hallway, she found him asleep on the sofa in the sitting room. He really was quite handsome, she decided. So different from the miners she was used to. His build was more slender, but there was an aura of strength about him, even sleeping. Right now, with his black hair all tousled from sleep, he had a vulnerable look to him.

Biting her lip, she wondered if she should wake him up. On the one hand, he couldn't be comfortable, but on the other hand he must have been very tired to be able to fall asleep there. Just as she decided to let him sleep while she checked on her mother, he spoke.

"I can hear your stomach rumbling."

"You can not!" Chloe's face heated with embarrassment.

"No, I can't," he admitted, opening his eyes and smiling at her. "But I could feel you debating about waking me."

"I'm sorry," she said, willing her heart to stop racing. "You should have woken me so I could have slept with my mother."

"No, I'm the one who's sorry." He sat up and stretched, and she couldn't help but notice the play of muscles under his shirt. "You were up early to be out with the search party, and then you put in a full day at the mine, and then I kept you up talking. I wouldn't have made it past supper after a day like that."

"I enjoyed talking with you." She enjoyed kissing him even more, but she wasn't about to admit that. To keep from making a fool of herself, she turned and led the way back to the kitchen.

"I'm afraid breakfast won't be nearly as elaborate as the dinner you made last night," she said. "We're running low on supplies."

"You don't have a food dispenser?"

She almost laughed at his surprise. "A food dispenser is a luxury item on Belspar. I get our food allotment from the supply depot, usually once a week or so."

He frowned. "They control even the food you're allowed?"

"It's a generous allotment, I've no complaints."

"Except now you have an extra mouth to feed," he pointed

out. "Isn't that going tax your resources?"

"It's fine," she assured him, placing a bowl of stewed fruit and grain in front of him. "We usually have more than we can use."

She could tell he wasn't happy with the situation, but they ate in silence.

"Perhaps when it's dark you can show me the cave your mother mentioned," Zephryn said when he was done eating.

"The cave's not safe," Granny said, coming out of Tierra's bedroom.

Chloe gasped, hand to her chest. She hadn't realized Granny was in the house. When had she arrived?

"Are you sure about the cave?" Zephryn asked with a frown. "Tierra said -"

Granny waved a dismissive hand. "Tierra hasn't been out of this house in years. Gannon found the cave more than a week ago, though he doesn't know who created it or how. He's set a watch on it to see who comes and goes."

The cave had been created by Chloe and her mother years ago. Tierra had claimed it was to test Chloe's abilities, but Chloe had always had her doubts. There was some other reason her mother had wanted the cave formed, perhaps as a place to hide if Gannon became too demanding.

"Then I'll have to return to my ship," Zephryn said. "Every day I'm here increases the risk of discovery. I don't want to be responsible for bringing trouble down on Chloe and her mother."

There was s snort from the old woman. "Your ship is buried under several feet of earth, thanks to this one," she nodded towards Chloe. "Gannon has a bug up his butt about something, there's patrols everywhere. It'd be even more risky trying to dig it up right now."

"Then I guess you're stuck with me for now," he said.

Chapter Ten

Chloe couldn't help feeling pleased at the prospect of Zephryn extending his stay under their roof. But the glow was short-lived and suddenly she was feeling shy again.

"I should take some breakfast to mother," she said, rising from the table.

"No need," Granny told her. "I left a plate on her table. I couldn't get her to wake up to eat but it'll be there for her later."

"You couldn't wake her?" Chloe repeated, trying not to show how worried that made her.

"Is that normal?" Zephryn asked.

Granny shrugged. "It's been an eventful few days, enough to throw anyone off."

Before Chloe could ask any of the thousand other questions she had about her mother's current condition, the old woman dusted her hands off on her apron.

"I have things to do," she announced. "I've filled your canister with my special tea. If you get the chance I'd appreciate it if you'd talk to my herb garden."

She was gone before either Chloe or Zephryn could say a word.

* * * * *

"Is she always that . . ."

"Odd?" Chloe finished for him. She laughed. "Mother always says Granny is as changeable as the weather. And she seems to get more so with the passing years."

"What did she mean about you talking to her herb garden?" Zephryn asked. He knew about gardens, but he'd never heard of anyone talking to one before.

Chloe held up the tea pot and he gave a nod. She refilled both their cups before sitting back down across from him. "In return for Granny's help, I use my gift to help the plants in her herb garden to grow."

"You can do that?"

"You look surprised. Have you forgotten already that I'm able to control the earth? According to you and my mother, that makes me an Earth Elemental."

"No, it's just unusual that you can both move the earth and manipulate plant life." It wasn't just unusual, it was extremely rare. Normally an Earth Elemental could do one or the other, not both. It took an incredible amount of power for them to be able to split their focus.

"Oh." Chloe caught her bottom lip between her teeth. "Is this a bad thing?"

"Not at all." He reached over and placed his hand on top of hers where it lay on the table. "It's part of who you are so it can be nothing but good."

A smile broke over her face, as he'd intended.

"I believe you're trying to flatter me."

"Is it working?"

"Maybe a just a little." Her smile dimmed and she withdrew her hand. "What was it like, growing up with people like you?"

"People like me?"

"Other Elementals." She stumbled over the word. "Not having to hide your abilities."

"Ah." He sat back in the chair. "For all that we were bred to become more powerful with each successive generation, and were given training to control our elements, we were not encouraged to use them. You recall I mentioned the inhibitors?"

She nodded, wide-eyed.

"To be perfectly honest, it was easy to forget that being an Elemental meant we had any kind of gift. All we had was our power rating." He held out his wrist and turned it over so she could see the numbers burned into the skin.

"What is that?" She reached out a tentative hand and touched the markings.

"WE-02-47-04 - Wind Elemental, second generation, forty-seventh result, power level four. That was my designation. The name I was known by in the compound."

"That's awful!"

"I was so proud of my power rating." He shook his head. "Power ratings were everything in the compound. So imagine our surprise when we arrived on Ardraci and discovered that our ratings meant nothing. An Elemental was judged on his ability to control his element, on how easily he could manipulate it, not how powerful he was."

"It must have been hard for you," she said.

"It was . . . disconcerting. So was seeing different Elementals in committed relationships."

"What do you mean?"

Zephryn shifted in his seat. "Every Ardraci is born with the potential for all four elements, but one is usually stronger than the others and when an Ardraci passes through *tespiro* the predominate one becomes their gift. Arjun was trying to isolate the gene sequence for each element so that his test subjects were born with the potential for one element only."

"That sounds horrible. But what has that got to do with—"

"I'm getting to that. To achieve this, Arjun created the breeding program so that Water Elementals would only have children with other Water Elementals, fire to fire, wind to wind, earth to earth."

She stared at him wide-eyed and he thought she was going to say something but she apparently changed her mind.

"So as a Wind Elemental, I was only with other Wind Elementals. My friend Ravi is a Water Elemental and he was only with other Water Elementals. When we arrived on Ardraci it seemed almost blasphemous to see a Fire Elemental with a Water Elemental, or any other combination of Elementals."

"And if I'd been born in the compound?"

"If you'd been born in the compound, we would have never met."

There was an adorable little frown on Chloe's face as she digested his last statement. "For what it's worth," Zephryn said, "I'm glad you *weren't* born in the compound."

Her gaze met his and then dropped again and a faint flush suffused her cheeks. He found that adorable too. Was this what Ravi meant when he told him it was the little things that first attracted him to Tasha? There was just something about

Chloe . . . he couldn't say what. But it was like she was a magnet and he was a lead compound. He wasn't sure what to do with all these new feelings, and he didn't like that one bit.

On the one hand, he definitely knew what he *wanted* to do. Bu on the other hand, he couldn't stop thinking about the story Ravi told him about the fire elemental, Pyre, and the tragedy that preceded his *tespiro*. He'd been with a girl in the barn the youth of his village commonly used for trysting. But the emotions had been too much for him and he'd lost control of his element. Both the barn and the girl he'd been with had gone up in flames. The only thing that saved him was the fact he was the source of the fire.

Chloe was no teenager, and her gift was just as powerful, if not more so, than Pyre's. There was no telling what might happen if her *tespiro* was triggered, catching them unaware.

"Chloe . . ." How was he supposed to broach the subject with her? He could really use Da'nat's help right about now.

The truth is always the best.

Zephryn gave a start. *Da'nat?* Then he realized what the Ilezie's voice in his mind meant. *Stop reading my mind!*

You must tell her the danger she faces. That we all face.

Are you sure she hasn't been through her tespiro? She has such a firm control of her element, despite being self-taught.

Her mother says she has not.

Zephryn hesitated, then, *Tierra's been sick for so long. Is it possible Chloe had such a mild tespiro that she underwent it without Tierra realizing it?*

Unlikely.

But it is possible. Da'nat?

But the Ilezie's presence vanished again. Zephryn ground his teeth together.

"Is something wrong?"

"No, sorry. Just something else I was thinking about." He sighed. "We need to talk about what your mother said, about me helping you . . ."

"Oh. That." She sat back in her chair, looking down at the table. "I don't know what mother told you about my little situation, but it's not exactly new."

"Little situation?" Zephryn was shocked. Between her power and her age, if she really was approaching *tespiro* it was more than just a little situation.

"I've been dealing with Gannon for years. I don't know why he's suddenly renewed his interest in me, but it's nothing I can't handle on my own."

"He's what?" A cold wind swept through the room before he could stop it. "What exactly has he been doing?"

Chloe's eyes widened as she watched a small whirlwind form on the table between them. "Nothing special," she replied, eyes captivated by the swirling wind. "But he's made his interest plain. And yesterday he asked me into his office for a glass of wine to celebrate my crew finding a rich vein of ore."

"Of course you refused," Zephryn stated flatly.

"What? No, of course not." She tore her eyes away from the spinning air to look directly at him. "When the mine master calls you into his office, you don't refuse." Her gaze was drawn back to the miniature whirlwind. "How are you able to keep it so contained?"

His brow furrowed in concentration and the wind dissipated.

"I'm sorry," he said a little sheepishly. "I usually have better control than that. But just the thought of this Gannon trying to take advantage of you . . ."

She shrugged. "Like I said, it's nothing new, but I'm surprised mother was even aware of it."

Zephryn hesitated, torn between wanting to find out more about what Gannon was up to and the need to clear the air about what her mother really wanted his help with. "Chloe . . ." He loved saying her name. It had such a beautiful cadence to it.

All at once he felt the mental equivalent to a slap in his head. Da'nat!

If you're not going to help, then don't eavesdrop, he told the Ilezie.

Then focus on the task at hand.

"Are you sure you're all right?" Chloe asked, concern on her face. "You keep wincing."

"Just a slight pain in the head," he said dryly. "I'm sure it will go away on its own."

"If you say so."

"Chloe, your mother isn't concerned about Gannon. At least, if she is, she hasn't mentioned it to me."

Her perfectly arched brows pulled together in a frown. "If it's not Gannon, then what does she think I need help with? It was me she was referring to, wasn't it?"

"Yes, it was." Though he'd grown up unused to alcohol in its many forms, if there was ever a time he could use a drink, that time would be now. "The thing is . . ." He sighed and ran a hand through his hair. "You've been getting headaches lately, haven't you? And they're getting worse."

"How did you—"

"And your control over your element has been slipping. I imagine you're having to be very careful outdoors, near any plants. Your gift has been getting stronger."

"It means something, doesn't it? Something . . . bad." The frown was replaced by a troubled look.

"How old were you when your mother created the cave?"

"The cave? I don't know - fourteen, maybe fifteen or sixteen?"

He nodded. It made perfect sense. "Do you remember when I talked about *tespiro*?"

"You said it was some kind of rite of passage, when an elemental's power manifests."

"The thing is, Chloe," he reached across the table and took one of her hands. "Your mother believes you never went through it."

Her hand tightened fractionally in his. "I don't understand," she said. "If I never made this transition, then how am I able to use my gift?"

"When a gift is strong enough it can sometimes manifest before *tespiro*. And it's even been known to delay it a year or two."

"A year or two," she repeated. "It's been more than a year or two for me."

"I know."

"This is bad, isn't it?" Her hand was cold in his. "Just how bad is it?"

Again he hesitated.

"Tell me!" The ground rumbled beneath them, but quickly stilled.

"It could be catastrophic."

Chapter Eleven

Her hand tightened in his before she tried to pull away, but he wouldn't let her. "On the other hand, it might be nothing at all," he went on quickly. "I've heard of cases where an elemental with a strong gift undergoes a mild *tespiro*. It's rare, but it has happened."

"Stop trying to shelter me from the truth!" She snatched her hand back and stood up. Wrapping her arms around herself as though she were cold, she spun away from the table and paced to the other side of the room. "You come here uninvited and suddenly my whole life is being turned upside down. My mother is not who I thought she was and I find out she's been lying to me for years."

The dishes on the table began to rattle as the ground began to shake.

"Chloe, I—"

"I need you to tell me what's happening to me, and how bad it's going to get. I need to know *why* this is happening."

It was the tears in her eyes that was his undoing. Zephryn got up from the table and went over to her, folding her in his arms.

"I don't have all the answers," he told her. "But I promise we'll figure it out together."

"What's going to happen to me?" she asked, voice muffled against his chest.

"We're going to get you through this," he said firmly. "I think that's what your mother created the cave for - it's a safe place for you to go through your transition. It helps if you're surrounded by your element."

"How bad is it going to be?"

He hesitated, but then spoke frankly. "I honestly don't know. I've never heard of anyone going through their *tespiro* after their gift has fully manifested. *Tespiro* is usually what triggers it."

"What else?"

Drawing her back over to the table, he sat her down beside him, keeping hold of one of her hands. "I won't lie to you. It's painful, sometimes it can be incredibly painful. It's not uncommon for someone in *tespiro* to lose control of their element."

She seemed to think about that for a moment. "Do you . . . do you think I am, the way I am, because mother was carrying me when she was in stasis for so long?"

Most certainly, Da'nat's voice whispered in his mind.

Are you sticking around this time or just going to keep buzzing in and out of my head?

There must have been an edge to his thoughts because he caught the sense of contrition from the Ilezie. *You must forgive me, my friend. The things unfolding on this world have been most unexpected. It has been most . . . unsettling.*

Da'nat? Was that an apology he'd just heard?

Rest assured we will do everything in our power to make sure

Chloe passes her tespiro intact, both body and mind.

"I think your mother's time in the stasis pod was definitely a contributing factor," he said out loud, quickly so that Chloe didn't think he was ignoring her.

"So it's true," she said bitterly. "I am just a freak."

"Just because you haven't undergone your *tespiro* doesn't make you a freak."

"You said this transition is where an elemental comes into their power . . ."

"Normally that's true."

"Just how much more power is it possible for me to have?" There was an edge of panic to her voice.

"I know a few very powerful elementals - that was the whole purpose of the breeding program you remember. There's a Wind Elemental, like me, only she wasn't part of the breeding program. But she's so powerful she can create windstorms that can lay waste to entire worlds. She can even harness the solar winds of space."

"Really?"

"One of my new friends is a Fire Elemental. He was able to stop a volcano by drawing the heat from it into himself. He was even able to tap into the world's core."

"What if I gain so much power I'm not able to control it?"

Da'nat?

It is possible she has already reached her full potential and will not increase in power.

But . . . ?

But it is also possible she will build up power until she implodes.

"You already control your power," he said, not wanted to

frighten her any more by giving her the full truth. "While it's common for someone's control to slip during *tespiro*, it's because until their gift manifests control can't be learned. So you've already taken the first step."

She will not fight this battle alone, Da'nat's voice whispered through his mind. *She will have you with her, and the Ilezie as well.*

* * * * *

Chloe gently extracted her hand from Zephryn's. "Thank you for being honest. What you've told me . . . it helps me understand what's been happening to me. I thought I was going crazy."

"I think you're very courageous," he told her. "I can't imagine having to deal with what you're going through without knowing the facts. But I don't understand why your mother never explained any of this to you."

"I can answer that."

They both started at the sound of Granny's voice from behind them. She seemed to delight in coming and going on a whim, just like an Ilezie.

Without waiting to be asked, the old woman seated herself at the table with them. "At first she thought she'd have more time, even though your gift was manifesting itself early. Then she just plumb couldn't find the words."

"But we've always been so close, why couldn't she just talk to me?"

"Would you have believed her? She was already getting a reputation for not being right in the head because of the sickness.

How could she expect you to believe the story of her escape from the breeding program and all those years drifting in space?"

Chloe looked down at the table. "Still . . . "

"When the change didn't happen and the years began to pass, she figured her time in stasis had done something to you. That you weren't going to undergo the transition." She shook her head. "I warned her, I did. No good would come of keeping secrets, the change would come whether she liked it or not. And the longer she put off talking about it, the harder it was going to be."

"It doesn't matter," Zephryn said brusquely. The only thing continuing to talk about it seem to accomplish was upsetting Chloe, and he hated to see her upset. "What's done is done. You know the truth *now*. That's what matters."

"Indeed," Granny said, then seemed to give herself a shake. "I came to warn you. Gannon's started to notice all the earth tremors we've had lately."

Chloe nodded. "Yes, he has some sort of equipment in his office that registers them."

"It don't just register them, it lets him track 'em too."

"You think he's going to track them to Chloe?" Zephryn asked. He really hoped not. Who knew what Gannon would do with that knowledge? Someone who could cause the earth to tremble would make a formidable weapon.

"If he hasn't already."

"Chloe . . . just how much does Gannon know about your abilities?"

"At first, mother tried to pretend I hadn't inherited any. But I slipped one time - I accelerated the growth of some flowers so

I could take her a bouquet. Someone saw me and reported it to Gannon."

He frowned. "I wouldn't think growing flowers would be of much use to the mine."

She sighed. "Mother was starting to become ill, and we needed the money. So when Gannon confronted her she admitted that I might have inherited some small part of her ability, but that it was more connected to growing things and detecting minerals."

"Which of course is very useful in a mining operation." He turned to look at Granny. "Does he know they're Elementals?"

There was just the slightest hesitation before she answered. "I don't think so, no. But I think he suspects she can do more than she says."

"What am I going to do?" Chloe asked, a faint edge of panic to her tone. It was to her credit there were no earth tremors.

"You learn control," Granny said bluntly. "You've done fine on your own, but you're mostly running on instinct. You need the boy to teach you how to use your gift properly."

Zephryn smiled faintly at being called a boy. "I'm not sure what help I can be, our elements are so different, but I can at least go over the basics with you."

"But not here." Granny was adamant. "You need to go underground. Maybe the old mine - no one ever goes there."

"That's because it was abandoned because it was so dangerous!" Chloe protested.

"Makes it all the better for your purposes. Don't have to worry about prying eyes."

"Sounds fine to me," Zephryn said. "But how do we get

there? You've both said it's too dangerous for me to leave the house."

"You wait until dark, of course."

"We'll need to get him a change of clothing," Chloe said. "Something that will let him blend in if we're spotted."

Granny nodded. "I'll take care of that. And I'll be back at sunset to sit with your mother." She pushed away from the table and got to her feet.

"Thank you," Chloe said.

"You can thank me by mastering your gift," Granny told her. "And not collapsing the whole mine while you're doing it."

Zephryn stared thoughtfully at the old woman as she left. He couldn't shake the feeling that she knew more than she was letting on. Where was she getting her information? The change would come, she said. Almost the exact words Tierra had used.

Chapter Twelve

Chloe had a thousand questions, all clamoring to get out at once, but she needed some time to herself to sort through everything Zephryn had told her so far. "Perhaps," she said tentatively, "this would be a good time for me to go to the supply depot for the food allotment."

Zephryn smiled, and she could swear she saw understanding in his eyes. "Why don't I clean up while you're gone?" he said, nodding towards the dishes in the basin. "It's the least I can do. And I can keep an eye on your mother as well."

His smile did funny things to her insides. She almost changed her mind about leaving, but he was already getting up. With a quiet sigh at her fancies, she pushed back from the table and went to her room for her jacket.

Chloe was two steps into the room before she noticed the neatly folded clothing on the bed. She frowned. Someone had been in here, but who? It couldn't be Zephryn, they'd been together the whole time since he'd awakened. Taking a closer look, she suddenly smiled.

She went back to the door and called out, "Zephryn? There's

something in here you should see."

He was wearing a puzzled frown as he approached, wiping his hands on a cloth. Apparently he'd wasted no time in starting the clean up.

"What is it?"

Moving aside so she wasn't blocking the door, she gestured towards the bed. "I don't know how she did it so quickly, but it looks like Granny left you a present."

His eyes lit up and he went over to the clothes, picking them up and shaking them out. "Thank the winds!"

He turned and caught her smiling. "What?"

"You said, 'Thank the winds.' My mother always praises the earth."

Zephryn smiled in return. "I guess it must be an Ardraci thing, praising your element. Thanking the winds was something I picked up on Ardraci. In the compound we weren't encouraged to think of a higher power or deity. Unless you counted Dr. Arjun as a higher power."

Chloe shivered. "He must have been a terrible man."

"He was. But he's gone now and all the rest of us can do is carry on." He held the shirt up to himself to check the fit. "I think she even got the right size. What do you think?"

"I think it takes very little to please you," she said with a smile.

He chuckled. "These ship suits are designed to be worn throughout an entire scouting mission, but that doesn't mean they have to be."

She reached for her jacket on its hook. "I shouldn't be long. Is there anything special you need?"

"Just for you to stay safe."

His words warmed her all the way to the supply depot.

The supply depot was a large warehouse, guarded by a former miner whose career ended with a cave-in that crushed his leg. He'd been the supply master for as long as Chloe could remember and they were great friends.

"Trust a Seeker to know when we receive a fresh shipment of bittersweet," he said by way of greeting.

"Really?"

He chuckled at her eagerness. "Just arrived this morning. If you hadn't shown up by tomorrow I'd have set some aside for you."

She gave the old man a hug. "You're too good to me, Orrin."

"If I was twenty years younger and not already married, I'd be a courtin' you, Miss Chloe."

That brought an outright laugh. "I happen to know you say that to every female under the age of sixty," she said.

"In case it's escaped your notice, there ain't that many of you."

"Mining's a hard life for a woman."

"Ain't that the truth," he said. "Still, it leaves you with plenty of men to choose from. When're you going to pick one to settle down with?"

"I don't know, Orrin. Next to you they all pale in comparison." Unbidden, an image of Zephryn popped into her mind. While the thought of settling down with one of the miners she worked with left her cold, the thought of being with Zephryn filled her with warmth. In her head she knew it was impossible. He didn't belong in the mining colony; he couldn't stay. But in her heart she dared to dream of the possibilities.

* * * * *

Still needing some time alone with her thoughts, Chloe took the long way home from the supply depot. Her path took her by Granny's tiny cottage and she stopped to have a look at the garden beside it.

It *did* look rather neglected. She felt a twinge of guilt - how long had it been since her last visit? Setting her parcels down, she took a step closer. Where should she start?

"Needs waterin'," a voice called out.

"Excuse me?" Startled, Chole turned, seeking out the source of the voice. She relaxed as she spotted Amira, Martin's wife, coming along the same path she'd taken.

"Those herbs of Granny's, they take more water than the rest of the plants. I try and get by to water 'em for her, but you know how it is." The woman shrugged as she reached the garden and stopped.

"I certainly do." Chloe turned her attention back to the garden. The row of herb plants along the front edge of the garden were just starting to bloom. "It looks like they're doing all right though."

"You must spend all of your spare time over here. I never see any weeds. Wish I could keep my own garden as tidy."

Chloe wondered what Amira would say if she told her the truth. That the reason there were no weeds in Granny's garden was because she asked them not to grow there. Would she believe her? Turn her in to Gannon? Demand that Chloe help her as well? She suppressed a sigh. It could be any of those things or something else altogether. She genuinely liked Amira. Not telling her the truth felt too much like lying.

"I remember even when you were little you liked to play around in the gardens. You were like a little flower yourself. You're a good girl, helping Granny out like you do."

It was Chloe's turn to shrug. "Weeding her garden is the least I can do, considering all she's done for my mother."

"How is Tierra these days?" Amira's concern was genuine; she and Tierra had been close friends when Tierra had been well enough to work the mine. In fact, they'd worked on the same crew.

Chloe sighed. "There hasn't really been much change," she said. "Her bad days are still out-numbering the good ones."

Amira shook her head. "That's a bad business, that. Ain't never heard of anyone taking so long to get over the dust sickness. Makes you wonder what good that fancy off-world doctor of Gannon's is."

"He does seem out of place here, doesn't he? And people still prefer to go to Granny with their problems."

"Granny's family," Amira stated firmly. "We're all family. We don't need no outsiders."

Maybe not outsiders like the doctor, Chloe thought. But she could think of at least one outsider who was welcome. "I guess it'll just take time. We were all outsiders at one time."

"There's those of us who'll always be outsiders, even some who're born here."

Chloe knew she was referring to Gannon. He may be the mine master, but he was not well-liked. It had been a shock when he was raised to master status instead of Martin.

"Well, I got no time for lolly-gagging. You give my best to Tierra."

"I'll do that," Chloe called out to Amira's retreating back.

Once Amira was out of sight, she went to the side of the garden where she couldn't be seen as easily, and knelt down. Laying her palms on the earth, she closed her eyes and breathed deeply. In and out, in and out. Her eyes opened again, but they were unfocused. Where earlier they had been a brown hazel, now they were so deep a green they practically glowed.

To the casual observer, the garden looked no different than the other small plots that dotted the community, Chloe was careful not to overdo it. If Granny's plants were a little greener, a little fuller, then it was only because she had more time to spend tending to them. But between the rows of vines, made tall by the stakes they encircled, the special herbs Granny used in her medicines flourished.

Chloe had learned to talk to the plants on her own, she ran on pure instinct. Tierra was able to show her a little of her gift for coaxing the earth to give up its gifts, but she'd fallen ill before she was able to show her daughter the true range of her abilities. Again, most of what Chloe knew of the earth she learned on her own.

Truth be told, she was looking forward to her lessons with Zephryn tonight. And not just because they'd be alone together. Tierra hadn't encouraged her to have any close friends, not that there were many children to be had in the mining colony, but she was all too aware that she was different from them. Now she knew the reason for it, but she'd grown up believing herself to be a freak. It was going to be wonderful to be with someone who was gifted as well, even if it was a totally different gift.

She couldn't help but wonder what Zephryn would be able to teach her.

Chapter Thirteen

Zephryn filled his lungs with fresh air and slowly let his breath out again. He took another deep breath, then another. The air didn't just fill his lungs, it rejuvenated his spirit. Turning, he caught Chloe watching him, a curious expression on her face.

"Being raised more or less underground means I've avoided the claustrophobia common to most Wind Elementals, but it still feels good being out in the open air again."

After Chloe returned with the provisions, she seemed peaceful and calm. They'd rested, she insisted on taking the sofa so that he could stretch out on her bed, until nightfall, when Granny arrived. Now he was having his first glimpse of the world outside her small house - more like a cabin from the size of it.

"Is it difficult for you when you are shut up in your space craft?" she asked.

"I don't know what it would be like cooped up in a cabin, or worse in a cargo hold, but when I'm piloting a ship I'm aware of the vastness of space surrounding me," he replied absently, looking around.

The house was set in a clearing of sorts, a sharply rising hill behind it and dense trees on either side. A path of white stone led from the house to a wider, packed dirt trail.

"You don't have a garden," he said, a little surprised.

Chloe shook her head. "We did when I was much younger, but once my gift for growing things began to manifest itself I found I couldn't always control the rate at which the plants grew. Mother decided it was safer not to have a garden at all than to risk someone noticing."

"Maybe we can change that," he said with a smile. Zephryn was finding it all too easy to smile around her. Something about her touched something inside him and made him feel . . . it made him feel things he was raised not to feel.

"We have a bit of a walk to the old mine," she told him. "We should get going."

He reached out and took her hand as she would have brushed by him. "So I don't lose you in the dark," he said, the picture of innocence.

She looked at him and he could see she was a little flustered by the gesture. There were two moons in the sky so the night was anything but dark. After a moment she shook her head slightly but didn't take her hand back as she led him down the path.

"Are you sure it's safe to stick to the path?" he asked. "Isn't there the danger of someone seeing us?"

She glanced over at him then back again. "Not really, no. We're at the end of this row of houses and the new mine is over there." She waved her other hand in a direction off at an angle. "We don't get many visitors."

The path petered out after a few more yards, but Chloe seemed to know where she was going. The trees began to thin out, replaced by outcroppings of rock. Two moons in the sky.

Zephryn couldn't help wondering if Chloe appreciated the romance of it all.

"It's not much farther," she said.

He held back a rueful sigh. Apparently her mind was on nothing but the business at hand.

Another few yards and she suddenly stopped, then pulled him into the bushes for concealment.

"Damn. I was afraid of this."

"What is it?" Peering over her shoulder he could see the mine entrance, lightly boarded up with a sign stating the mine was closed and no admittance.

"Those," she said, pointing at what looked to be two floating globes, flashing red and yellow lights. "They're security spheres. They'll be set to activate and record if anything larger than a small animal approaches the mine."

Zephryn studied the spheres. They seemed to be self-propelled - nothing was tethering them in place. "I think I can take care of them," he said. Drawing his winds to him, he let them loose again, pushing the spheres gently away.

"That was amazing!" Chloe's voice was filled with admiration. "Your wind was so precise, moving the spheres and nothing else. You must have a great deal of control."

He couldn't help feeling a little puffed up by her praise. "It's the kind of control I hope I'll be able to help *you* with."

Wasting no more time, Chloe led the way into the mine. The boards were just a minor obstacle. It was easy enough to climb between them. Zephryn paused and swallowed hard. Inside the mine it was pitch black. He could almost feel the press of the earth around him.

"Are you all right?" Chloe asked, her hand seeking his again.

At the touch of her hand, he immediately felt grounded once more. "It's just a little dark in here, that's all."

"Don't worry, I came prepared." She snapped on a hand held light. "We only need to use this until we get to the main chamber. There's a master panel for the lights in the mine proper."

"Won't someone notice a power drain if we put the lights on in the entire mine?" He followed her into the bowels of the mine.

"They're powered by solar collectors. There's probably a surplus of stored energy, just waiting to be used."

There was nothing more to be said until they reached the large, spacious main chamber.

"Perfect," Zephryn said, as Chloe turned on the lights.

"Where do we start?" Chloe asked.

They were deep enough in the old mine that there was no chance of being interrupted. Zephryn could think of a number of things he'd like to start, but with an effort he focused on the task at hand.

"Most of my training involved learning to use my element," he said. "And then to control it. Maybe we should do a series of tests to see just what you can already do with your gift."

"All right. What do you want me to do first?"

"Let's start with something simple. Part of your gift is your affinity to plants, have you ever tried to deliberately make them grow?"

"Yes, sometimes I enhance the plants in Granny's garden, but only when she's running low on her herbs. And I caused plants to grow on the spot under which your ship is buried."

His poor ship! How was it ever going to take off again? "What about making them grow other places, like inside this mine, for instance."

"I—no, there's never been a need. I don't know if I can. Plants don't normally grow so far from the surface."

"Why don't you give it a try?"

Chloe turned her attention to the ground in front of them. Zephryn could almost feel her concentrating.

"Relax," he said softly, so as not to distract her. "Let it come naturally."

There was a slight movement in the ground in front of them and a plant pushed its way upwards, it's dark leaves unfurling as it grew. It didn't stop until the buds opened and blue flowers appeared.

"That's perfect," he told her, meaning every word. "Now let's see what else you can do. What's your job in the mine?"

"I'm a Seeker. It's my job to find the veins of ore and then to guide the crew in following them until the vein is no longer profitable."

"Have you ever tried to do more than just locate these minerals?"

Her brows drew together in a frown. "I'm not sure I know what you mean."

"If you were to reach out with your gift and locate a specific metal, could you bring it to you instead of having someone dig it out?"

"I—I don't know. I've never tried such a thing."

"I'm willing to bet you're able to." He gave her an encouraging smile and she closed her eyes to concentrate.

"There are traces of many different metals," she said after a moment. "Copper, zinc, gold - but not enough of any of them to make it worth keeping the mine open."

"That's all right," he assured her. "We don't need a lot. Focus on one of the metals, the gold say, and try drawing it towards you."

Within a matter of seconds, tiny nuggets of gold began appearing, pushing up from below, forming along the walls, dropping from the ceiling like rain, until there was a double handful at her feet. Chloe opened her eyes. "That was incredible!"

"It certainly was." He grinned at her. "All right, let's try something a little harder. When you're feeling strong emotions - anger, fear - your control slips and you've been causing tremors."

It wasn't really a question, but she nodded anyway.

"I want you to deliberately try and make the earth move, just a little bit."

"But what if I lose control?" She looked alarmed at the prospect.

"You won't," he said with more confidence than he felt. He smiled reassuringly at her. "Trust me."

She looked long and hard into his eyes. "All right."

Again, she closed her eyes. At first the tremor beneath them was barely noticeable, then it grew stronger. There was a sudden upheaval that sent her careening into him. Her eyes snapped open and the tremors abruptly stopped as they crashed to the ground - Chloe on top.

"I'm sorry," she gasped. "I didn't think it was strong enough so I tried . . . why are you looking at me like that?"

Zephryn's arms had automatically gone around her as they fell. He wasn't even aware of the hard ground beneath him, only the warm woman on top of him. She fell silent. Slowly he reached up and cupped the back of her head, drawing her face down to his. Their lips met and Zephryn thought he'd never tasted anything so amazing. Her lips parted in a surprised "Oh" and he took full advantage.

It took all of his self control not to roll them over so she was beneath him. After a few minutes she pulled away and looked down at him, eyes wide and maybe just the tiniest bit unfocused. "No one's ever kissed me like that before," she whispered.

"I'm sorry, I—"

"Kiss me again."

Her lips were on his again before he could form the words to tell her what a bad idea this was. And then it was too late, he no longer cared that it was a bad idea. All he could focus on was her taste, her smell, the feel of her in his arms.

"Oh!" Chloe raised her head and looked around them in wonder. "I guess I still need to work on my control."

"Not on my account," Zephryn mumbled.

She giggled. "Not that, silly. Look around us."

Reluctantly he let her go, giving her one last quick kiss before shifting so he could rise up on his elbows. Where before the ground had been hard packed earth, now they were lying in a bed of flowers. The lush pink blossoms were streaked with red and gave off a heady scent.

"That's so strange," Chloe said. "I've never seen this kind of flower before. I wonder where they came from?"

Before he could stop her, she'd buried her face in the fragrant blossoms. "They smell amazing!"

Zephryn's eyes widened. He'd seen these flowers once before, on Ardraci. He and Chloe were in serious trouble.

Chapter Fourteen

Da'nat came out of his meditative state with a shiver. Something was not right. He gave a very un-Ilezie like snort. Of course something was not right. Nothing about this mission was right. Not the energy they'd been sent out to track, not this planet . . . They should have sent someone more experienced with Zephryn, someone who was used to the vagaries of space.

He was young, by Ilezie standards, with only ten syllables to his name. Far too young to have been sent on such an important mission. But the Ilezie were not a prolific race, there were too few of them and they were spread far too thin.

You are far too hard on yourself.

He started at the whisper in his mind.

You've done well, thus far, but the true test for the girl will not be at your young friend's hands. You begin to realize that, don't you?

There was power in the voice. Power and something far greater. The Ilezie were impervious to temperature extremes, but he felt a sudden chill. *Who are you? What do you want with me?*

I want to help. I have been helping, but I thought it was time to introduce myself.

Who are you? he repeated.

You may call me Gra'anna.

Da'nat reeled in shock. Impossible! Gra'anna had disappeared millennia ago, lost in legend and time.

Not lost, my young friend, merely misplaced.

The colour leeched out of him. Only the most ancient of the Ilezie could read the thoughts of others, not meant to be shared, with such ease. He stared wildly around - all at once the ship seemed claustrophobic. Waves of soothing energy filled him, calming him. Gra'anna.

"Why have I not sensed your presence?" he whispered, too shaken to mind-speak.

I did not wish it.

Even now the presence was masked. Da'nat was grateful he was already sitting down, it saved him the embarrassment of collapsing in the presence of an ancient. "What did you mean, the true test for the girl will not be at Zephryn's hands?"

The voice took on a dream like quality. *So much has been forgotten over the centuries, the Prophecy twisted and changed. The Gifts were not meant to stagnate, but to grow and change. In this respect, Uri Arjun was right, though his methods were untenable. All these centuries searching for the One. So unnecessary.*

"I don't understand. Why do you say the search was unnecessary?

They were never meant to be sought, only found when the time was right. The truth is just now coming to light.

It was not by chance the Ilezie had become caretakers of the Ardraci. It was the Ilezie who bestowed the elemental gifts on them. The reasons for this were lost in time, but for millennia the Ilezie had been testing the Ardraci for the One, the Ardraci who would save not only the Ilezie home world, but the universe itself from disaster.

"Yes," he said. "We have begun to realize there is more than just One."

Five. It is five who will be One. Chloe is the last.

"Five? Are you sure?"

The Wind brought a world back to life; the Fire set events to be into motion; the Water has the power of both life and death; the Earth shall fill the empty spaces; and the Spirit will bind that which is broken.

"We . . . we have no Elemental Spirit," Da'nat whispered.

The Spirit is already in place. It will manifest when the time has come.

"Why are you telling me all of this?"

So that you may tell the others.

Da'nat jumped to his feet and began to pace. "But you're an ancient. Surely—"

Events have made me weak. I am . . . not as I was. You will see when we meet.

"How did you get here?"

I followed a prophecy.

His steps took him over to a chair and he sank down into it. "We were not sent here for scientific study, were we?"

No.

"Why?" The question slipped out before he could stop it. He kept expecting to be censured for his audacity.

The bonds are essential to our survival. You have bonded with Zephryn, he will bond with Chloe.

97

Da'nat frowned. He genuinely liked the boy and did not wish to see him coerced. *What if he does not wish to form a bond with her?*

Gentle laughter filled his mind. *Even were she not one of the Five, their paths are destined to merge.*

What about the energy force we were tracking?

The bonds it forges are essential as well. It has already been bonded with Wind and Fire and Water. Now it must bond to Earth.

And just how is it going to do this? Is this part of Chloe's test?

There was no answer.

Inside the small ship buried beneath the earth, Da'nat paced. An Ilezie was at all times calm and serene, in full control of their emotions. He was none of those things. He felt like a small child.

He was suddenly reminded of Zephryn, and the young man's irritation when his questions were left unanswered. He now knew just how he felt.

Gra'anna had set out with four others on a quest from the Ilezie home world more than a millennia ago. If the specifics of that quest had been recorded those records had vanished, but none of them ever returned. It had always been assumed they'd been lost to the Great Vortex.

Had this planet, on the edge of nowhere, been her destination? Or had it been chance that brought her here? But in either case the bigger question was why. Why would she seek this planet out, and if she did not, why would she stay if she were here by accident?

All Ilezie were capable of self-teleportation in varying degrees. Young ones, like himself, could only teleport short distances, such as in and out of this ship, or with much effort as far as the cottage belonging to Chloe and her mother. But older Ilezie could travel much further. He knew of several who could travel from planet to planet in an emergency, although this took a great deal of energy. But an ancient would be able to travel the universe without a ship - such was their power.

Unconsciously, his pacing brought him to the door of the room he'd been assigned to on the ship. He went in and adopted a meditative position on the padded platform that served as his bed. This scattered thinking needed to stop. He would meditate until he regained his equilibrium. It was unseemly for an Ilezie past his hundredth year to be so fretful.

But he couldn't seem to shake off the effect his conversation with Gra'anna had on him. *They were never meant to be sought, only found when the time was right.* Did those who sent him on this quest with Zephryn know this? No, he had to believe the others were in the dark as much as he had been. His first priority had been the energy pulse, finding Chloe had been happenstance. There would have been no reason to hide such knowledge from him . . . or was there?

Again, he wished someone older had been sent on this mission, someone with more experience. At the very least, someone with enough power to send a message to the nearest Ilezie to let them know what was happening. Though his mental abilities were strong, they were not strong enough to pass through the security shield.

He would have to wait. He would summon the patience the Ilezie were famous for and let events play out as they would before he and Zephryn left this place. If Chloe was indeed the Earth Elemental needed to stand with the others, she would be coming with them and he presumed Tierra would be too. Would Gra'anna wish to come as well? It would be crowded in this little ship, but they could signal ahead to have the Valkyrie meet them.

Casting his mind's energy towards Zephryn to see how he was faring, the Ilezie's eyes widened with his second shock of the day.

The true test for the girl will not be at your young friend's hands.

He could only hope that Gra'anna was right, otherwise they were all going to be in serious trouble.

* * * * *

As Chloe inhaled the exotic scent of the pink blossoms, she was suffused with a wonderful lassitude. Dimly she was aware that she was still on top of Zephryn and he was saying something to her about moving, but she stayed where she was. She *liked* where she was.

"Chloe, you have to stop." He tried to pull her away from the flowers. "The pollen from these flowers . . . just trust me on this. You need to stop inhaling it before it's too late."

She finally focused on his face. He looked agitated. "You've seen these flowers before, haven't you?"

"They're called passion bells. They're common on Ardraci, wherever an Earth Elemental lives. They appear whenever . . . that is . . . their scent is laced with . . ." A shiver went through him as she waved one of the blossoms under his nose.

"There, now it's too late for both of us."

"No! It's not too late. Not as long as at least one of us has a shred of willpower left. The effects wear off quickly, but I need you to get off of me first."

She gave an experiment wriggle and he fell back with a groan. "Stop that! You're killing me here."

"Why don't you let me kiss it and make it all better?"

"This isn't you talking," he said, a little desperately. "It's the passion bells."

"I didn't know flowers could talk," she said with a giggle. Her skin tingled and an unfamiliar warmth filled her. She deliberately rubbed herself against him again.

"Stop! It's the flowers making you feel this way. Their scent is laced with a powerful aphrodisiac."

"Maybe I don't care." She leaned down and kissed him. For a moment he returned her kiss, then he tried to push her away.

"Well I do! This isn't what we came here for."

Chloe stared down into his eyes. "Are you going to deny there's some kind of connection between us? I know you've felt it too."

He remained silent and she smiled in triumph. "That's what I thought."

Chapter Fifteen

There was a part of Chloe that had known, without Zephryn telling her, what the flowers were and why they'd emerged. Her mother had told her about the passion bells around the time she developed her first crush on a boy. She'd been so disappointed when they hadn't appeared, but Tierra had comforted her by telling her the boy in question just wasn't special enough.

Of course Tierra's explanation left out the fact the flowers would only appear to an Earth Elemental, she'd said they only appeared to 'special' people like them. Chloe had no doubt Zephryn had seen them on the planet Ardraci, but it was unlikely he knew everything she did about them.

Her smile faded as she looked down at him. People were always underestimating her because of the way she looked - too young, too pretty, too delicate. Zephryn was like everyone else, mistaking her innate shyness for innocence and naiveté. But Chloe knew what she wanted, and what she wanted right now was Zephryn. Let him think she was overcome with lust because of the passion bells, there would be time enough to sort out their feelings for each other later.

She lowered her head until their lips were almost touching. "Relax," she whispered. "This won't hurt a bit."

"Chlo—"

Whatever he was about to say was cut off as she kissed him. And she kept on kissing him until he started to kiss her back.

"That wasn't so bad, was it?" She trailed a series of kisses along his jaw.

"Just remember," he said, a little short of breath, "That I tried to do the right thing."

"My ever so noble spaceman," she agreed, going to work on the buttons of his shirt.

He placed one hand over hers to stop her. "Are you sure about this?"

"Very sure." She was beginning to find his nobility tiresome. Was he always this slow?

To prove her sincerity, she lifted herself off of him and got to her feet. Slowly she began removing her clothing, only a little self-conscious under his heated gaze. When she was finished, Zephryn raised himself to his knees.

"You're so beautiful."

The reverence in his tone made her tremble slightly. There was no doubt that he wanted this as much as she did. He wrapped his arms around her and pulled her closer, kissing her belly, then her navel.

"I can smell your arousal," he said, just before his head dipped lower. "I've wanted to do this since I first saw you in nothing but your towel."

She held on to his head to keep her balance as he gently pushed her legs further apart. His hands were hot on her skin as he parted the delicate folds between her legs, and she couldn't hold back a moan as his tongue dipped and swirled, causing sensation to build on sensation. It was almost more than she could bear, but she cried out in disappointment when he finally lifted his head again.

"Why did you stop?" She flushed at the neediness in the question.

He lowered her slowly back down to the bed of flowers. "Because I need to be inside you."

The rough quality of his voice made her shiver. "Yes." Somehow, that was exactly what she needed too.

Zephryn quickly divested himself of his clothing but she had little time to admire him before he was lying beside her, stroking her breast, her stomach, raised up on one elbow so he could watch the path his hand was taking.

"So very beautiful," he said.

"Please," she begged. At this point she wasn't even sure she knew what she was begging for, all she knew was that she needed him to keep touching her.

He leaned over and kissed the underside of her breasts, his hand coming up to tug on one aching tip as he took the other into his mouth, biting gently. The sensation shot straight to her fiery core. Her back arched in response and her breath began coming in pants.

"Zephryn!"

Ignoring her pleas, he continued to lavish attention on her breasts, lifting his head to kiss her mouth as well. Finally, finally! He moved between her legs, but then stopped.

"Last chance," he told her, breathing heavily, obviously

holding on by a thread. "If we go any further I won't be able to stop if you change your mind."

"I won't change my mind!"

Zephryn stared into her eyes for a moment, then kissed her. A long, lingering kiss that she felt throughout her entire body. Then, bracing himself with one hand, he used the other to guide his cock inside her aching sheathe. They both moaned.

He was bigger than she expected, but he was slow and gentle, and her body stretched to accommodate him. Too slow, too gentle. She needed hard and fast. Arching up to meet him, Chloe wrapped her legs around his waist, urging him to go faster.

"Zephryn, please!"

He seemed determined to torture her with his slow, steady strokes. Chloe ran her hands over the skin of his chest and up to his shoulders. It was like touching warm spider silk.

"I'm not made of glass," she gasped, rising to meet him. "Please!"

Zephryn drove into her, his mouth coming down on hers with bruising force. Chloe opened readily for him and their tongues dueled in tandem with his thrusts. Too soon she felt her body begin to tighten and she cried out, spasming around him. Another two strokes and Zephryn followed, thrusting deep and filling her with his essence.

He slowed and stopped, breathing heavily, head bowed. Somehow he managed to turn them so he was on the bottom and she was draped bonelessly over him. She sighed, too spent for words, and rubbed her head on his sweat dampened shoulder. Zephryn's arm tightened around her and her eyes closed, a smile of utter satisfaction on her face.

* * * * *

Chloe sighed. It felt so perfect, lying sated in Zephryn's arms. She never wanted to move. But much as she'd like to, they couldn't stay like this forever. They had to get back to her mother's house before it started getting light out. She had no idea how long they'd been in the old mine, but it felt like hours. They needed to move. In another moment or two.

Zephryn stirred beneath her. "Chloe . . . we can't stay here like this," he said, echoing her thoughts. "We—"

He broke off what he was saying and she raised her head to see what had caught his attention. There was a puzzled look on his face as he looked around. "I don't understand . . ."

"What—" The rest of what she was about to say ended in a yelp as he suddenly sat up, dislodging her. "Zephryn!"

"Sorry," he said absently, looking intently around them. His brows drew together in a frown. "How are you feeling?"

"I was feeling perfectly fine. Wonderful, in fact, until you—"

"No surges of power? No loss of control?"

"What? No. Zephryn, what's going on?"

"I don't understand it," he muttered, getting to his feet. He offered her a helping hand and she accepted, getting to her feet as well.

"This—" He looked down at her suddenly. "This wasn't your first time with a man, was it?"

"No, it wasn't." She bristled a little at the intensity of his stare.

"Maybe that's why there was no reaction." He seemed to be talking more to himself than to her.

"I'm sorry if you were disappointed," she snapped, any lingering warmth evaporating.

He ignored her comment about being disappointed, and that smarted. She began pulling on her clothes, eyes stinging. "Well you needn't worry about it happening again. I promise I'll keep my hands to myself from now on."

That seemed to snap him out of whatever he was focused on. "Oh, Chloe. No. Forgive me." She stood stiffly as he wrapped his arms around her. "How could anyone ever be disappointed in you?" he asked, voice muffled as he buried his face in her hair. "You were wonderful, perfect."

"Then you don't mind that you weren't my first?" she asked, thawing just a little.

"Of course not. Just so long as you don't mind I've been with a great many women, because of the breeding program."

She turned her head so she could kiss him. It didn't last nearly long enough, but she didn't want to start anything they wouldn't have time to finish.

"So just how many women have you been with?" she asked as he turned away and began dressing.

"I don't know, exactly. Records were kept so I could find out if it's important to you."

"It's not," she said, shaking her head. Definitely not. "I was just curious. But a breeding program . . . that must mean you have children."

He sighed and pulled her into his arms again. "Yes, but I've never met any of them. Contact between family members was forbidden."

Her heart went out to him. It was hard for her to imagine the life he led. "What had you so bothered when you woke up? It seemed like you were expecting something."

Now he hesitated and she started getting a sinking feeling in the pit of her stomach, though she couldn't have said why. She pulled back to look up at him. "Zephryn? Talk to me."

"It's nothing really." He wouldn't meet her eyes.

"In my experience, nothing usually means something."

"It's just . . ." He let go of her to run a hand through his hair. "It's just, I thought you haven't been through your *tespiro* yet, and strong feelings . . . what normally happens . . . that is, it was to be expected . . ."

Chloe pulled away from him completely, needing some distance between them. "You thought that our being together would trigger this *tespiro* you and Granny were talking about. In fact, you were counting on it, weren't you?"

"No! I mean, yes, but not the way you think."

"And just what would you know about what I think?" she asked bitterly. She felt betrayed, not so much by Zephryn, but by her own foolish heart. "You were just using me, trying to force this change on me."

"No!" He reached for her but she evaded his grasp. "Chloe, I'm sorry I jumped to conclusions, but I'm not sorry for what happened between us. It was special, and whether you've been with anyone else or not before me, or been through your *tespiro* or not doesn't make it any less special."

"I'd like to believe you," she said, and to her surprise she meant every word. "I just . . ."

He stepped closer and this time she let him. "I don't understand how I can care so much for someone I've known for such a short time, but I do." Gently, tentatively, he reached out a hand to draw her closer. "I knew from the moment I first saw you that you were special. You talked about a connection between us . . . I feel it too."

"You do?" Chloe's hurt and anger seemed to drain away.

"Yes." His head dipped down and he kissed her once, twice, a gentle touching of the lips. Chloe melted into his arms. The ground beneath them began to shake.

"I said I was sorry," he said, pulling back to look at her. His face was a picture of sincerity.

"I believe you," she assured him. "Whatever is causing the earth to shake, it isn't me."

Chapter Sixteen

The rumbling got louder, becoming a roar as the earth shook beneath their feet.

"Cave in!" Chloe shouted over the noise, grabbing Zephryn and holding on. "The mine's collapsing."

There was no time to run. The lights went out and Chloe braced herself for impact, burying herself in Zephryn's arms. But the impact never came. After a moment she lifted her head and realized he'd created a whirlwind around them to keep the worst of the debris away. But the vortex was faltering.

Pushing outwards with her mind, she was able to join with Zephryn's wind to keep the earth at bay. It seemed like forever but was only a few seconds more before the earth was still again. They were safe inside a pocket of space created by their combined power. Zephryn's wind had even kept the dust at bay.

"Are you all right?" Zephryn asked.

"I - yes, I think so." Chloe reluctantly loosened her grip on him. "I don't understand why this happened though."

"Could it have been triggered when I had you trying out your powers?"

"No," she shook her head, even though he wasn't able to see it. "If it was something I did I would have felt it immediately and been able to stop it. This was something else."

Kneeling down, she placed her hands flat on the ground and reached out with her mind. She sent her thoughts deep into the earth, frowning as she began to piece together what had caused the cave-in.

"I was right, this wasn't natural. There was an explosion in the main tunnel."

"An explosion? But why?"

"I don't know." Chloe stood upright again. "This mine is used to train new workers, Gannon wouldn't give the order to collapse it like this without a really good reason."

"So you think someone else tried to blow it up?"

"I don't know what to think," she said honestly.

"I have an even better question. Do you think whoever set off the explosion knew we were in here?"

Chloe shivered at the thought of someone deliberately trying to bury them alive. "But why?"

"I don't know."

She could hear him moving around.

"What are you doing?"

"Just checking to see how big a space we have. I need to see if I can replace the air in here so we can keep breathing."

"You can do that?"

She could hear the smile in his voice when he answered. "Don't you know by now? I can do all kinds of things."

He brushed up against her and she shivered again, but this time for a different reason. "How long before they send out a rescue team?" he asked, breath hot on her neck as he spoke right into her ear.

"There won't be one," she said, voice laced with regret. "No one knows we're here, remember?"

"No one but whoever caused the explosion."

Chloe didn't answer. She reached out with her senses again, this time following the path to the mine entrance.

"The earth around us isn't tightly packed. I think . . . I'm sure I can force a pathway to open for us to escape."

She felt his hands brush against her again. This time he drew her in for a kiss. "For luck," he told her.

Chloe reluctantly left the comfort of his arms and turned to face the way out. "Stay close behind me. I don't know how long I'll be able to keep the tunnel open. I've never tried anything this big before."

"I'm in your hands," he told her. She was humbled by his trust.

It took a great deal of focus and concentration to coax the rock and dirt to withdraw, opening up a pathway. Even though she was used to working in enclosed spaces, it was unnerving work. There was no light to see, they had to feel their way. The tunnel she created was not large, and it collapsed behind them as they inched their way along.

When it started to become difficult to breath, Zephryn called the air to them. Apparently he did his job a little too well because by the time Chloe broke through to the outside they were a little giddy from the oxygen rich air they'd been breathing.

"We did it!" she said, hardly able to believe it.

"You mean you did it. My hero," he said, wrapping his arms around her and kissing her thoroughly. "Although you're a mighty dusty looking hero."

She mock punched him in the arm. "C'mon. We'd better get out of here before we run into someone. I'm sure Gannon will have dispatched a team to investigate."

Zephryn hesitated, looking back towards the mine.

"What is it?"

"I just wish we could do a little investigating. Maybe find some evidence the mine was tampered with."

"And do what with it? It's not like we can take it to Gannon."

He sighed. "You're right, of course. I just . . . "

"Just?"

Shaking his head, he said, "Never mind. Let's go home."

Hand in hand, they followed the path that led them back to the cottage.

* * * * *

They were being watched. Zephryn didn't know how he knew, he just knew it with a certainty that went right to his bones. He felt it as soon as they left the mine. Not wanting to alarm Chloe, he kept the information to himself, although he kept a sharp eye out as they travelled back to her house.

She was exhausted from the effort of digging them out. Her control of her element was still far from perfect, so she used more of her personal energy than she should have. He needed to get her home and settled into bed, then he could come back to see what he could find out about the cave-in.

He desperately needed to speak with Da'nat.

Granny met them at the door. "What happened?" she asked the moment she saw them.

"Mine collapsed," Chloe said wearily, pushing past her, Zephryn right behind.

Zephryn gave a shake of his head and Granny reined in whatever else she'd been about to say. He kissed Chloe on the forehead and steered her towards the hall. "Why don't you use the shower first. I'd say you earned it."

She was too tired to argue, just nodded and continued on down the hallway. Granny went back into the sitting room where she'd been waiting for them and Zephryn followed. He was a little tired himself and didn't want to take the chance of nodding off if he sat down, so he leaned against the wall near the door.

"What happened?" Granny asked, once Chloe was out of sight. "Did she . . . "

He shook his head. "It's not what you think. Chloe did fine. She did great, as a matter of fact. But afterwards . . . someone set off an explosion to cause a cave-in."

"Are you sure it wasn't natural?"

"Without seeing the evidence I can't be sure of anything. But Chloe's sure, and that's good enough for me."

Granny nodded in agreement.

"It just doesn't make sense," Zephryn continued. "Why would someone want to collapse the mine? Unless . . . unless whoever it was knew we were in there and wanted us out of the way."

She appeared to mull that over for a moment. Her next question surprised him. "Were you seen?"

"Yes," he said, running a hand through his hair, shaking some dust loose. "But not until afterwards. There was no one around when we went in, I'm sure of it. Just as I'm sure there was someone out there when we came out. Call it a sixth sense if you will, but I can sense these things."

"I believe you."

"But why would anyone want to harm Chloe?" he burst out. "It doesn't make any sense."

"Maybe they weren't trying to harm her," Granny said thoughtfully. "Maybe someone wanted to test her."

"Test her? You think Gannon knows what she is?"

Granny shook her head. "No, whoever it was it wasn't Gannon. It was too subtle for him - he's more the confrontational sort. No . . . this was someone else. Something else."

Zephryn pushed away from the wall. "We need to get to the bottom of this. I have to go back there."

"Not so fast." Granny held him back with her tiny hand on his arm and he was shocked by her strength. He couldn't have broken her grip if he tried.

"You need to stay right where you are. Where it's safe. If anyone's going to go snooping around, it should be me."

"You? But—" He stopped as she tightened her grip until he felt each bony finger dig into his arm.

"Don't forget, Gannon's still looking for you. This is a closed community, strangers stick out."

"But you don't —"

"Don't know what to look for?" She snorted. "This ain't my first space flight, sonny. I know exactly what to look for. Probably better than you do."

Finally letting go of him, she pushed past him to the door.

"Now you go on and get cleaned up. I got work to do."

She was gone before he could make any further protest. Zephryn rubbed his arm where she'd held him. He wouldn't be surprised to find bruises there later. There was something not quite right about that old woman, but he couldn't quite put his finger on what it was. Maybe Da'nat would have some insight on that as well.

If he could make contact with him.

Chapter Seventeen

Zephryn closed his eyes as the warm water cascaded over him. This was the one thing he missed when travelling in his scout ship, a proper shower. In the quarters he was given on the *Valkryrie* the shower had choices - sonic, micro, or water - but the scout ship was outfitted with a micro shower. He hated the sensation of the microbes spilling over him, even if they weren't visible to the naked eye. They made his skin tingle and he never quite felt clean enough when they were done.

Opening his eyes again he stared down at the marks on his arm and frowned. The pinkish red lines were darkening, and still tender to the touch. He wouldn't have believed Granny was capable of such strength, she seemed so tiny. But then the Ilezie were small creatures as well and he knew from experience just how strong they were.

Chloe was asleep by the time he emerged from the bathroom. He smiled to see she'd left enough room in the bed for him, if they cuddled closely . . . but his smile turned to a sigh and he turned resolutely away. He had to speak with Da'nat and it was best done in another room so he didn't wake her.

He went to the sitting room in the front of the house and stood in the center.

Da'nat? he projected as loudly as he could with his mind. *We need to talk.*

"There is no need to shout," a mild voice said from behind him.

Zephryn whirled, adopting a defensive posture, then slowly straightening up again as he saw the Ilezie. "I wasn't shouting. I used my mind, as you prefer," he said with a frown.

"Think you not a mind can shout? Then I have not trained you nearly as well as I believed."

"Fine! I apologize for shouting." A light breeze ruffled through the room. "But it can be damned difficult to get your attention at times."

"Now it is I who must apologize." Da'nat gestured towards the sofa. "Sit. You are weary with more than just your thoughts."

Irritation slowly dissipating, Zephryn did as he was bade.

"I have not been myself," the Ilezie admitted. "Our stop on this world was unexpected, as have been the events unfolding here. I am unused to such . . . disorder."

"I think you should know . . . that is, Chloe and I . . ." He ran a hand through his hair, searching for the right words.

Da'nat came as close to smiling as he'd ever seen him. "Though I fully understand it was not your intention, I know what occurred when you tested Chloe in the old mine."

Zephryn tried, and failed, to fight off the flush that suffused his face. "So why didn't it trigger her *tespiro*? You said—"

"It appears I was mistaken." Da'nat paced away and then turned again. "When an Ardraci approaches *tespiro*, their . . .

psyche, if you will, is opened up to all the possibilities of their elemental gift. Their body, of course, is not equipped to handle such a thing which is what causes the upheaval of mind and spirit. Those who are able to adapt go on to become fully functional Elementals. Those who cannot . . . die."

"And Chloe?"

"I believe that because of Tierra's extended period of time in stasis, Chloe was born with her psyche already opened."

"I don't understand. Are you saying she was born already undergoing her *tespiro*?"

"In effect, yes. But because she was so newly formed herself, her body and mind were able to adapt as she grew. There was no upheaval because she is adapting as she ages."

"Wait a minute." Zephryn straightened up where he was sitting. "If what you're saying is true, then that would mean she's been in *tespiro* since she was born."

"That is correct."

"But . . . during *tespiro*, we gain in power. If she's been in *tespiro* all this time . . . "

"Then she's been gaining in power her whole life. The tremors she was inadvertently causing were not from a loss of control, but from a leakage of her power."

Zephryn paled slightly, trying to imagine a lifetime of accumulated power. "Just how much power is one Ardraci able to hold?"

"I do not know," Da'nat admitted. "But I fear she grows close to her limit. I will do what I can to help her, but whether it will be enough . . ." he shrugged. "Expelling power, such as the amount needed to collapse the mine, is actually a good thing."

"It wasn't her."

"Pardon?"

Shifting in his seat again, Zephryn looked over at the Ilezie. "Chloe had nothing to do with the mine collapsing. Someone set an explosion." After being shaken to the core by these new revelations about Chloe, he had only a faint sense of satisfaction of seeing Da'nat shaken by the news of the mine explosion. "I wanted to investigate myself, but Granny thought it would be too dangerous so she's going to see what she can find out."

"This is bad," Da'nat said. "This is very bad. But the old woman is correct. You should not be found alone outside of this place."

"But what about Chloe? She has a shift in the mine tomorrow. Maybe I should—"

"I do not believe she will be in any danger during the day. I have observed these miners, they are like a family and will protect her."

"If you say so," Zephryn said dubiously. He stifled a yawn.

"You are weary and need your rest. I, too, will see what I can learn of this mine collapse. We will talk again tomorrow."

Zephryn could have sworn he only closed his eyes for a second, but when he opened them again the Ilezie was gone. Though he chaffed at the thought of others doing what he perceived to be his job, he knew, deep down, it was too risky for him to be seen. That would only bring trouble down on Tierra and Chloe. Not that they weren't in a world of trouble already.

* * * * *

Chloe felt an unfamiliar warmth at her back and a heavy weight pressing down at her waist. Memory returned and she smiled.

Zephryn. She'd meant to stay awake for him, but despite her best efforts she'd fallen asleep. Waking up like this was something she could easily get used to.

With a resigned, but quiet sigh, she moved his arm off of her and wriggled her way out of bed. As much as she'd like to spend the day with him, she had a shift at the mine. Laying his arm gently down, she made sure to cover him back up and then grinned as he stirred faintly, frowning in his sleep.

Dressing as silently as possible, she gave Zephryn one last, lingering glance and then went out to the kitchen to grab a bite to eat. Considering all they'd been through, she felt good. Amazing, as a matter of fact. There were a thousand things she wanted to say to him, to let him know it wasn't just the passion bells at work back in the mine, but it would have to wait until later.

She checked on her mother, who was sleeping peacefully, and then made her way to the mine. The rest of her team mates were just assembling.

"Good morning!" she greeted them.

Martin's brows rose at her cheerful tone. "You're in an exceptionally good mood. I thought you didn't like the morning shifts."

"Maybe my good mood accounts for me making an exception this time," she said amiably.

"Maybe someone got lucky last night," Wayland snickered. He was the youngest team member, even younger than she was.

She stuck her tongue out at him.

"Hey, Chloe. You live at the end of the row . . . did you hear the explosion at the old mine last night?" Farley asked, tightening his tool belt.

Chloe froze in the act of adjusting her own. "Uh, explosion?"

"I warned Gannon that old mine wasn't safe, even for training," Martin said, shaking his head. "It's just lucky there wasn't a training team in there when it collapsed."

"I hear Gannon's fit to be tied," Spenser chimed in. "It weren't no natural cave-in."

"What else could it be?" Chloe asked. Though she appeared casual, her heart was racing a mile a minute. There hadn't been a trace of the security spheres when they emerged from the old mine, but that didn't mean they hadn't been close enough to pick up their images.

"Maybe that's what all those tremors we've been feeling have been about," Wayland suggested. "It was that old mine getting ready to let go."

Spenser shook his head. "Sophie, from the office, said nothing showed up on that fancy equipment of Gannon's. Just boom - it collapsed."

"You thinking explosives?" Martin asked with a frown. "Why would anyone want to do that?"

"Could be someone from Black Thunder," Farley suggested. "Heard they ain't doing so good."

"But what could they hope to gain?" Chloe asked, for the sake of argument.

"Stirring up trouble, same as always."

There were five mining territories on Belspar. The largest was Hammer Dome, with Righteous Angels and Black Thunder vying for second and third place followed by Arcland, and then Lightning Strike trailing the pack. As resources on Belspar slowly started to deplete, the competition between mines increased.

Harlan's eyes lit up. "You think Gannon's going to organize a raiding party? Been a long time since we had ourselves a good old raid."

Chloe bit her lip. She certainly hoped not. It would be terrible if the explosion sent Gannon on the warpath. What happened wasn't her fault, nor Zephryn's, but she'd feel guilty all the same. She couldn't help the nagging feeling that if they hadn't been in there, the explosion would have never happened. Or maybe it would have. Maybe it was just a coincidence.

"Don't talk foolish," Martin snapped.

His brother had been killed in a raid, Chloe remembered. It had been a winter raid, a few years prior, and the supply ships had been late coming. Raids were almost necessary for survival at that time, but once everyone was re-supplied the mine masters met and reached an agreement to halt the raiding.

"Gannon give you any grief over that young pup Ulrik?" Spenser asked Chloe, deliberately changing the subject.

"Ulrik?"

The others chuckled. "That newbie you put in place right before our big strike."

"Oh," she said, a little relieved. "Not a word, why?"

"Saw him going into Gannon's office early on - heard Gannon's been closeted with him ever since."

Chloe's eyes widened. "I wonder . . . do you think he had something to do with the mine collapse?"

"I dunno. But something's going on. That's for sure."

Could this Ulrik have been responsible for collapsing the mine, knowing she and Zephryn were in there? It seemed a little extreme just to get back at her for a prank.

More importantly, she wondered if he'd been lurking around the mine when she and Zephryn emerged. Just how much could he have seen? She had a sinking feeling in the pit of her stomach, and it stayed with her through the end of her shift.

Chapter Eighteen

Zephryn woke with a frown on his face. He knew Chloe had a shift in the mine today, but he'd hoped to see her before she left, maybe have the opportunity to talk with her... It was important that she know what happened between them meant something. It wasn't just a result of the passion blossoms or trying to trigger her *tespiro*.

He found another set of clothes, similar to the ones he'd been wearing the day before, folded neatly on the chair. Chloe? Or Granny? It didn't matter, he appreciated the gesture. He'd have to ask Chloe about a cleaning processor when she returned, he was accumulating quite the pile of soiled clothing. There was one on the ship, but it was a little hard to reach right now.

Just thinking about her brought a smile to his face. He couldn't wait for his friend Ravi to meet her. He was going to love her.

His smile dimmed a little. That was assuming Chloe would want to leave here with him. It would be a tight squeeze, but there would be room for her mother on the scout ship as well. Surely with all the medical knowledge aboard the *Valkyrie* there would be a cure for her mother.

Slowly he sat down on the bed again. But here Chloe had friends, her work at the mine, all the earth an elemental could want . . . If she came with him, all she'd have was . . . him.

"You're thinking too much, boy." Granny's voice came from the doorway.

He looked up, startled. "How —"

She snorted. "I could see it on your face. Already worrying about the future, ain't ya?" Shaking her head, she turned from the door and headed towards the kitchen. "I made tea. Might as well drink it while it's hot."

With a resigned sigh, Zephryn got up to follow her. Just as well she'd interrupted before his thoughts started circling like a ship on a tight orbit. This is what happened when he was left with too much time on his hands and too little to do.

"First off," Granny said without any preamble as he sat down at the table. "Chloe was right. That weren't no natural mine collapse. There were explosives went missing from the stores warehouse, and traces of them were found in the debris."

"Do you find out who set them off? Or why?"

"No, more's the pity. Someone was very careful to cover their tracks. I don't like it." The old woman shook her head. "I don't like it at all."

"You said before about someone testing Chloe . . . how likely is that?"

"About as likely as someone wanting to do the girl harm."

He stared at her. "Are you saying you think it was an accident? That whoever set off the explosion didn't know we were in there?"

"I'm saying I don't know! There ain't none of it makes sense."

She rubbed her forehead and took a deep breath. "We've got a bit of a problem."

"Just one?" He reached for one of the steaming biscuits on the plate in the center of the table. They were already buttered and seemed to just melt in his mouth.

"It's Tierra. I can't seemed to wake her."

Zephryn looked at her in alarm. She didn't have to tell him how bad that was. "What happened?"

"It's been coming on gradual like. She's been sleeping longer, awake less often and for shorter periods of time. Chloe mentioned it to me just before you crashed here."

"What can we do for her?"

For the first time since he'd met her, Granny looked uncertain. "The best thing would be to get her off world and into a proper medical facility, if it's not already too late. Barring that . . . I just don't know."

Chloe was going to be beside herself. "Do you think Gannon's doctor might be able help?" he asked slowly. He hated to think what Gannon might want in return, but this was Chloe's mother they were talking about and he knew she'd do anything for her.

"I'm not altogether sure he's not the reason she's like she is." She pinned him with her intense stare. "She's not better, she's not worse, she just won't wake up. I can't find anything wrong with her. This is not part of the lung sickness."

"Do you think Gannon would have his doctor give her something? Like what, poison?"

"I believe that man is capable of anything."

"But why? What could he hope to gain?"

"Why Chloe of course. He knows her mother is her weakness. If he can control her mother's health, he can control Chloe."

"There's a stasis pod on my ship," Zephryn said slowly. "If we can get her there . . . at least she'd have a chance . . ."

"I was hoping you'd say that," Granny said, her relief evident. "But such a thing will need to be carefully coordinated. If Gannon were to catch us . . ."

From what they'd told him of the man, if Gannon caught them, they'd end up dead. And Chloe worse than dead. "How long will you need to get organized?"

"Two, maybe three days." The old woman rose from the table.

"So I guess it falls to me to tell Chloe what's happening." This was not what he was hoping to greet Chloe with when she got home. On the other hand, the sooner they were off this world, the better off they'd all be.

"Knew you'd turn out to be good for something, boy."

* * * * *

The closer she got to the end of her shift in the mine, the twitchier Chloe became. She couldn't shake the feeling that someone was watching her, although that would be impossible in here. Or at least it should be. Glancing surreptitiously around, she saw she wasn't the only one who seemed ill at ease. Farley kept adjusting and readjusting his light, Wayland would stop every few minutes to check his progress, shake his head, and carry on.

The position of the new vein allowed for drift mining and Gannon had authorized a new adit to access the mine, even though it meant drilling ventilation shafts every few hundred feet. The tunnel snaked its way into the side of the hill, following the ore. The vein was thicker here than the end further into the mine, which is why they were coming at it from this side.

"Damn cheap bastard," Martin muttered.

"I presume you mean the mine master?" Chloe asked with a grin.

"Sure, he'll authorize a new adit, but he won't make it wide enough so's we can bring in the heavy equipment to make our lives easier."

"We're not paid for easy," she pointed out.

"That's for damn sure!" Farley said with a snort.

"Anyone else feel that?" Spenser asked suddenly.

"Feel what?" Martin asked. He signalled everyone to stop what they were doing. As crew chief these workers were his responsibility and if even one of them was feeling like something was off . . .

"Sorry, boss. I just got this feeling. It's like . . ."

"Like a feeling of impending doom?" Wayland asked in a sotto voice.

Chloe mock punched him in the arm. "I thought I was the only one feeling this way," she admitted.

"Gather 'round people," Martin ordered. "I've been feeling like something's off since we stopped for our lunch break. Anyone else?"

There were nods and murmurs of agreement from the rest of the crew, most admitting they didn't say anything because like Chloe they thought they were alone in feeling so.

"I thought it was just new mine jitters," Farley said. "Same's I get every time we start a new one."

"Yeah, but this time it felt different," Spenser said. "Almost like —"

That was as far as he got before the sound of an explosion filled the small space. Shoring timbers cracked as the ceiling of the mine collapsed. In the confined space there was no place to run, even if they'd had time. A cascading shower of rocks slammed into the small group.

Chloe acted on instinct, pushing upwards and outwards with her mind to keep the worst of it from crushing them. She made the protective bubble as large as she was able and could only hope that it encompassed everyone.

The rumbling and shaking seemed to go on forever but in reality couldn't have been more than a few minutes. As the dust began to settle, Chloe started to let go of the bubble, but quickly firmed it up again when the rock began to shift without her support.

Martin coughed, then asked, "Sound off. Is everyone all right?"

One by one the crew sounded off, from oldest to youngest. They reported assorted scrapes and bruises, and Spenser thought his arm might be broken. Only two voices were missing, Wayland and his partner Pavric.

"Feel around people, they got to be here somewhere." It was dark as sin. The only one wearing a light on their miner's hat had been Farley and he lost it in the collapse. Everyone else depended on the lights strung along the tunnel, lights that were broken during the cave-in.

"Got one here," Harlan said after a few precious moments passed. "Can't tell which one, but he's breathing."

"Can you tell how badly he's hurt?"

There was another pause. "Arms and legs seem sound, but the side of his head's wet. Probably got hit by a rock."

"Got the other one over here," Farley called out. "Least ways I found his boots. Rest of him seems to be under a shoring timber and a whole mess of rock."

Chloe felt tears prick at the corners of her eyes. If only she'd been faster, better able to control her gift, they might have been able to make it out of the danger zone, if not the adit itself.

"All right, everyone," Martin said. "We all know the risks of the job, and some of us have even been here before. The only thing we can do is sit tight until they dig us out."

"What happened?" Harlan asked. "Was that an explosion I heard or just the noise from the support beams giving way from a tremor?"

"Sounded like an explosion to me, before all hell broke loose," Spenser put in.

"Now stop that right now," Martin said. "No sense speculating before we know the facts. It'll fall to Gannon to figure this out."

"Gannon," Harlan scoffed. "Did you see the substandard timber he used for shoring? He's probably the reason we're in this mess."

"Stop talking." Martin snapped. "You're wasting air. This space is small enough without you using up all its air with this crap."

"But—"

"Enough!"

Chloe wondered if there was anything to what Harlan said. It would be just like Gannon to use less than quality material, just to save a few dollars. He probably didn't waste the money doing a land survey on this side of the mine either. It might have told him that the area wasn't stable enough for drift mining.

Keeping the protective bubble steady, she reached out with her senses to see how bad the cave-in was. Her heart sank when she realized just how far back the collapsed tunnel went. There was no way their air was going to last until the rescue crew reached them.

Chapter Nineteen

Zephryn found the day passing with agonizing slowness. He was no longer used to spending hours doing nothing. Although even when he lived in the compound he wasn't exactly idle. When he had no breeding duties, he would spend hours at his computer console doing research, taking a break every now and then to work out in one of the exercise rooms. And he had an extensive collection of data cubes for entertainment.

He checked on Tierra a few times, but there was no change. It was just as Granny had said - she was no better and no worse, she just wasn't waking up. He trusted the old woman was right and they'd be able to find help for her off-world. Hopefully this coma-like state she was in didn't mean it was too late.

Finding a data reader in the front sitting room he checked it out, grinning when he found a romance novel already loaded and half read. There were a couple more data cubes on the table where he found it, two more romances and a technical manual.

With a sigh he set the reader down again. What chance had he for any romance once Chloe came home and he had to tell her about her mother? Of course romance should be one of the last things on his mind, under the circumstances, but he just couldn't seem to help himself. Every time he thought of Chloe he thought of the future, with her in it.

Using his wind, he picked up one of the small crystals from the shelf and spun it in lazy circles. Though it looked simple enough, it took a great deal of concentration and he was rather proud of his skill. Da'nat had been insistent that he learn to fine tune his gift in such a way.

"Any fool can create a whirlwind," the Ilezie told him, "But it takes a master to narrow the focus of a single breath of air. Are you a fool, or a master?"

Fortunately, he had no bad habits to unlearn when it came to using his element. It had been suppressed when he was in the compound so it had only been since his release he was able to use it at all. Once he was able to create a stream of air fine enough to pluck the top off a flower, Da'nat had him try hardening the air.

"I don't understand," Zephryn had said.

"When you interact with the air, it is not the air itself you control, it is the molecules within the air. If you focus on these molecules and bring them closer together, the resulting air will become denser."

It took Zephryn several tries before he was able to "see" these molecules Da'nat spoke of, but once he did he was able to push them closer together to create a wall of air. It was invisible to the naked eye, but could be felt as a resistance. He continued to practice this as well until he could create a wall strong enough to stop a person from moving forward, though he could not keep up such density for long.

"Not even Nakeisha, for all her power, is able to do such," Da'nat told him.

And Zephryn realized that had been his point all along. He'd been comparing himself to the Ardraci Ambassador, whose power was unrivaled, and was left feeling inadequate. After all, he'd been bred for his power, hadn't he? Da'nat had tried to tell him each gift was unique in itself, but he hadn't understood until then.

He sighed. And none of this was helping with his boredom right now. Looking around the small sitting room, he wondered when Chloe found time for any leisure. Looking after her mother, working in the mine, taking care of their home . . . when did she have a chance to relax?

There was at least one of these things he could help her with. Determined to give her a pleasant surprise before her unpleasant one, he got up and searched for some cleaning supplies, finding them in a small closet just off the kitchen. Cleaning was something else he was good at, just like cooking. He'd clean her house for her and then prepare a feast. Or at least as much of one as her larder would allow.

Several hours later it was with a sense of satisfaction he put the last of the cleaning supplies away again. The place was spotless. The only thing he hadn't been able to take care of was the small pile of soiled clothing and linens he'd gathered. Staring at the offending pile on the floor, he wondered what he should do with them. If Chloe and her mother had a refresher, it was well hidden.

"They need to be done by hand," Granny said from behind him, as though she could read his mind.

"You do have a way of just popping up out of nowhere," he said, annoyed at the start she'd given him. "And what do you mean, 'done by hand'?"

"There's a laundry cart comes around once a week. Anything more and you need to wash it yourself with soap and water in a basin."

"Oh." It sounded pretty primitive to him.

"People did it that way for hundreds of years," Granny assured him. "But that don't matter none, I—"

The wailing of a siren could be heard in the distance.

"What's that?" Zephryn asked. It had a distinctly different sound than the one that marked the beginning and end of the shifts in the mine.

Granny didn't answer for a moment. In fact, he wasn't even sure she'd heard his question, she was staring off into the distance, a blank look on her face. He opened his mouth to ask again, but before he could she spoke.

"It means there's been a cave-in." She said reluctantly.

"A cave-in, another one?" Zephryn moved towards the door. "I have to go make sure Chloe's all right."

The old woman clutched at his arm. "It's too dangerous, you need to just stay put. Let the others take care of it."

"Not this time." He shook her hand off. "If Chloe's been caught in another cave-in, I need to be there for her."

"You leave me no choice, boy." Granny gestured with her hand and he slumped to the ground. "I'm sorry, boy," she said, looking down at his unconscious form. "But I can't afford for you to get caught out there. Not when we're so close."

"Close to what?"

The voice came from behind her and Granny turned slowly to see Da'nat standing there. He'd been drawn by the sound of the siren, also ready to stop Zephryn from rushing to Chloe's aid.

"Damnation," Granny said.

* * * * *

It was getting hard to breathe. Dust sifted down through the protective barrier Chloe had erected and she firmed it up. In a way it was ironic. They were safe as long as she kept the barrier up, and because she drew her strength from the earth around her she could keep it up indefinitely, but it wasn't going to do them any good when the air ran out.

They were buried too deep to hear the cave-in siren. She wondered if Zephryn had and if her mother was awake to tell him what it meant. It was selfish, she knew, but she wished he was with her right now, and not just because he could have drawn fresh air to them.

"Sound off," Martin said, wheezing.

They'd been keeping conversation to a minimum, to conserve air, but Martin was having them sound off every few minutes to make sure everyone was all right. This time only Chloe and Harlan answered his call and Harlan was just barely conscious.

From the time her gift first started to manifest, Tierra had drilled into her the necessity of keeping it a secret, that their very lives could depend on no one knowing what they could do. As a small child it had seemed like a game, having this secret just between the two of them, but when she was a little older she had a harder time dealing with it.

"But we can do so much to help in the mines . . . we could be rich if we did all the work ourselves."

"That's not how it works, baby girl," her mother had told her sadly. "I know it's hard, but no one must ever know what we can do. It would be the end for us both."

At the time she'd pouted, only seeing the benefits, and the rewards. But as she grew to adulthood she understood the wisdom of her mother. Now she could think of no way of escaping without exposing what they were, what she could do. The earth above them needed too much shoring up. They could never break out the way she and Zephryn had and not be discovered.

"You know, one of them earth tremors wouldn't go amiss right about now," Martin said. "Just something to cause a line to the surface. Nothing too big, just enough so's it looks like the air hole came natural."

"What?"

"Do you really want to die in here, when we both know you don't need to?"

Chloe stared in the direction of his voice. "How did you know?" she whispered.

"I weren't born a miner, like most. I seen a lot of things in my travels, heard stories . . . "

"But . . . you never said anything."

"Nothing to say. Weren't my secret to tell." She could picture him shrugging. "Might have said something under the old mine master, but Gannon . . ."

"Martin, I—"

"Best do it quick, afore it's too late," Martin said. His voice was just a thread as he added, "If you can't trust your crew, who can you trust?"

Who indeed? These men were family - brothers, uncles . . . Martin was the father she never had. The earth would sustain her until she was found but her secret would be exposed just the same. Could she really have just let them die here when she had the means to save them? She'd like to think in the end she would have dug them out regardless of the consequences to herself.

Creating an air vent . . . it was the perfect solution. Why hadn't she thought of it herself?

She sent a tendril of awareness questing outwards, probing for a fissure that would lead to the outside. It took several false tries, and took longer than she would have liked, but she found one that with only the slightest manipulation could be extended down to their chamber.

The tricky part was actually feeding it through the earth above them. She had to push the soft earth to the side and harden it to keep it from filling in again. As Martin had suggested, she gave the earth a slight shake for good measure. How else to explain running out of air and suddenly being able to breathe again?

"It's done, Martin," she said. "Martin?"

There was no answer. Just as well. She knew they were going to have to have a long talk about this, but she'd just as soon it wasn't now.

Chloe took a deep breath. Fresh air mixed with stale, but nothing had ever felt so good. It would take some time for it to completely replace the air in the chamber, but for now it was enough. It would keep them alive.

By the time the rescue team broke through, the rest of the

crew was awake again, including Wayland, who was barely coherent from his head injury. Cheers went up from the crowd as the rest of the crew followed his stretcher out under their own power. The onsite medical team gave a cursory look at them, advised them to take a five-day rest, and spirited Wayland away.

There was much joking about naming Martin's team the Miracle Crew for having survived.

"You don't know the half of it," Harlan said to anyone who would listen. "Our air was all but gone. Then there was this tremor just as I was passing out. When I come to I could breathe again. That there tremor opened up an air vent."

"And the way that debris formed a pocket around you all . . ." One of the rescue crew shook his head.

"No miracle about that," Martin said gruffly. "Just pure luck the way the support beams fell."

The damage assessors were just about to enter the adit when the ground trembled slightly and the sound of the collapsing tunnel was heard.

Chloe was as surprised as anyone and gave her head a slight shake when Martin turned and caught her eye. Then his gaze drifted to someone behind her and she turned to see Gannon approaching. Panic filled her. She couldn't deal with him. Not right now at any rate.

She started to push through the crowd, angling away from him. Martin took a few steps over to block the mine-master's path.

"Gannon. I'll be wanting a word with you."

"It can wait," Gannon told him, eyes focused on Chloe's retreating figure.

"No, it can't. It's about those shoring beams . . ."

Clearly frustrated, Gannon finally looked at the crew chief, taking in the grim expression on his face.

"Fine!" he snapped. "In my office."

Martin breathed a tiny sigh of relief. At least he'd bought Chloe some time. But he had a sinking feeling that careful as she'd been, her secret wasn't going to be a secret much longer.

Chapter Twenty

"What are you?" Da'nat asked, eyes fixed on the old woman.

Granny turned slowly around. "I am no one to be trifled with."

"You're not human, that much is certain," he continued, as though she hadn't spoken.

"No, I am not," she admitted. "But I was, once."

"And now?"

"And now it does not matter. Things are moving faster than I'd anticipated. I—"

Da'nat took a step closer. "I ask you again, what are you?"

"I don't think you're ready to know," she said. She raised a hand to forestall his next question. "Not yet. I'll tell you everything, but you're going to have to have a little patience."

"All right," he agreed, after a moment. It wasn't as though he had any choice. "Then tell me why you rendered my companion unconscious."

Granny snorted. "For the same reason you teleported in here, to stop him from going after Chloe. Oh, yes," she added, at his startled look. "I know all about teleportation."

Da'nat wasn't quite sure what to make of the creature before him, there was something both very alien and very familiar about her. He could not read her, and that in itself was disturbing.

"What did you mean when you said you couldn't afford for him to be caught out there, not when you were so close? Close to what?"

"To the end of this phase of my life," she said with a sigh. She gestured towards the table. "We might as well be comfortable. He's not going anywhere. At least not right now."

He was not a creature used to following another's orders, but Da'nat found himself sitting down at the table.

"You knew about Chloe and her mother, their gifts," he said. "How?"

"You'd be surprised at some of the things I know," Granny said dryly.

"What kind of things?"

She sighed. "Forgive me. I don't mean to be deliberately mysterious. It's just . . . it's been a long time since I've seen one of your kind. Not altogether sure if I can trust you."

"And yet you think I should blindly trust you?" Da'nat asked, unable to hide his astonishment.

"You're not very old, not for an Ilezie, are you?"

"How could you possibly know that?"

"'Cause I know what true age is."

"Enough of this!" Da'nat did something he had never in his life done before. He lost his temper. "What do you want from me?"

Granny's eyes widened, just a fraction. "I want to help, that's all. I want to help Tierra get well. I want to help you and your young friend escape this world unscathed. But most of all, I want to help Chloe reach her full potential."

"And how exactly do you propose to do all that?"

"By making sure events play out as they were meant to."

"You're a Seer, aren't you?" he asked suddenly. Though many of the Ardraci were able to see into the future, their powers were insignificant next to a true Seer. Very few races could boast of a Seer, a soul with the rare ability to not only see into the future, but to follow the paths of events as they branched out into different possibilities, like roads leading to different destinations.

"That's one of my talents, yes," she admitted.

"And what gives you the right to meddle, to take control of this future?"

"The right of my visions! Do you think it's so easy, being a Seer? I see all of the paths and possibilities, all of them! I see which paths lead to death and destruction, which to pain and loss. And though the possibilities are endless, I know which ones will lead to the fewest casualties. It has always been so."

"I know who you are," Da'nat whispered suddenly.

"Good! Then I'll expect you to help me." Granny looked at him fiercely, suddenly seeming larger than her tiny frame.

"What do you want me to do?"

"You'll start by taking your friend, here," she nodded towards Zephryn, "to his ship. He'll be safe from discovery and it'll keep him from going after the girl."

"What do I tell him? Is she . . ."

Granny closed her eyes briefly. "She's safe. They'll have her out eventually. But you need to leave now."

"Why? I—"

"Gannon's sending his men for Tierra."

"Then we'll take her to the ship too. She—"

Granny was already shaking her head. "No. She needs to be here when Gannon's men arrive. I don't like it, but he won't dare hurt her, and she's the catalyst for what's to come."

Da'nat merely nodded. Rising from the table, he stood over Zephryn's prone body and they both disappeared.

"I hope you know what you're doing, you old fool." Granny said, then she, too, vanished.

* * * * *

Chloe's feet were dragging by the time she made it home. It was almost dawn. She was exhausted both mentally and physically. She still couldn't believe Martin had figured out what she was, although they hadn't had an opportunity to talk about it so she really had no idea how much he knew.

A five day rest! A smile curved her lips. A bath, a good sleep, and still plenty of time to get to know Zephryn better. Her smile dimmed a little. That was provided he felt the same way. They hadn't really had a chance to talk since their . . . encounter.

Her quiet life had been turned upside down lately. There were so many questions to be answered, like who had set off the explosion that trapped them in the old mine, and why. And the cave-in at the new mine . . . had it really been because of the shoddy shoring materials, or was something else going on. And Gannon . . . why was he suddenly showing so much more interest in her? Other than the obvious reasons.

She definitely needed to talk with Zephryn. And Granny. Maybe it was time to unbury his ship, at least enough for him to get inside to assess the damage. When she first rescued him, her mother said something about using his ship to escape, it would probably be a good idea for her to take part in the conversation as well.

Opening the door she frowned. She was sure she'd locked it. Shrugging off an uneasy feeling, she went inside, shedding her dust covered jacket as she did so.

"Zephryn?" she called.

It was a little surprising, and if she was honest with herself disappointing, that he wasn't waiting for her. She'd told him she'd be back in time for supper and here the sun was rising. Without a doubt he'd heard the siren and must have wondered what it meant - at the very least wouldn't he have wondered why she hadn't returned when she said she would?

Maybe Granny had stopped by to explain what was happening. But that still didn't tell her where he was now. Continuing down the hallway she called again, but there was still no answer.

Poking her head into her bedroom as she passed, she checked to see if he was sleeping but the bed was made and there was no sign of him. Surely he hadn't been foolish enough to venture outside? She supposed if he had, as long as he was dressed in the clothes Granny had found for him, no one would notice another face in the crowd. But still . . . it was a stupid, if not dangerous, thing to do.

She nearly tripped over a pile of clothes and bedding in the kitchen.

"Laundry?" she said aloud. "You were going to do the laundry?" She gave a laugh.

The man was a never ending mystery. But the mystery of where he had gotten to was one she needed to solve as soon as possible.

Her eye was caught by her mother's door. It was standing open. It was never left open. Chloe felt the first true chill of fear. She knew better than to believe her mother could have done it.

Slowly she approached, afraid of what she might find.

"Mother!"

The bed was empty, the bedding pulled off to the side as though in a struggle. The small table beside the bed was overturned and the lamp was on the floor, broken.

"Zephryn? Answer me!"

A cold fist clutched at her heart. She couldn't bring herself to believe that Zephryn had anything to do with her mother's disappearance, but what else could have both of them vanish?

"I'm sorry," Granny said from behind her.

Chloe spun around, tears filling her eyes. "What happened?"

"We heard the siren and he wanted to go after you. I couldn't have that."

"Granny, what did you do?"

The old woman's chin lifted. "What I had to do. He's safe," she added hurriedly as the ground began to tremble as though reflecting Chloe's rising anger. "He's just a little . . . incapacitated for now."

"And my mother?"

"I'm not sure," Granny said unhappily. "When I came back, she was gone."

Her remaining strength seemed to leave her and Chloe sank down onto one of the kitchen chairs. "Where's Zephryn?"

"Back on his ship." Granny was unapologetic. "In fairness to the boy, he didn't go by choice. I may have had to knock him out a little."

Chloe never thought to wonder how Granny could have accomplished this, nor did she need to guess who had her mother. Obviously Gannon sent his men for her while she was trapped in the mine. Were the two events connected? Could Gannon have caused the cave-in to keep her from stopping him?

"I need Zephryn," she said with quiet determination. "He can help me get mother back. And then we can leave this place once and for all."

"You don't—" Granny stopped what she was about to say as a strong gust of wind rattled the windows of the small house. Neither of them had been aware of the rising storm outside.

"What is it?" Chloe asked.

"I'd say your beau is awake," Granny said dryly. Another burst of wind slammed into the house. "And he ain't happy."

Chapter Twenty-one

Zephryn woke from the strangest dream. It took him a moment or two to reorient himself to the here and now. He blinked several times to clear his vision and sat up.

"I must be still dreaming," he said.

He was in his bed on the scout ship. How by all the winds did he get here? The last thing he remembered was . . . it all came back to him in a rush. The cave-in siren, Chloe, and . . . "Granny!"

"The one you call Granny is not here," said Da'nat from the doorway. He was looking as calm and serene as ever, no outward sign of the turmoil his thoughts were in.

"Da'nat! What the hell's going on?" Zephryn got to his feet and stalked over to the door, towering over the Ilezie. Da'nat was not in the least bit intimidated. "Why am I here?"

"It was for your own protection."

"My protection? What about Chloe? What about her protection?"

"She is safe. She is in her home."

"Then I need to go to her." Zephryn pushed past the alien easily and headed towards the hatch.

"That would not be advisable," Da'nat said, behind him now.

"I don't care what's 'advisable'," Zephryn said, placing his palm on the hatch's locking mechanism. "I'm going to see Chloe and you're not going to stop me."

The door slid open to reveal a wall of earth. A few loose stones and clumps of dirt fell inside the ship. "What kind of game are you playing?"

"I, more than anyone, know this is not a game. But as you see, you cannot go to her."

"No? Watch me!"

Zephryn created a small whirlwind between himself and the door. It spun faster and faster, confined in place. Then he began feeding it with air molecules, thickening it, making it denser and denser still. When he judged it to be of sufficient strength, he tipped it, sending it point first into the barrier in front of him.

"This is not wise—" Da'nat tried to warn him.

"I don't care."

The whirlwind acted as a drill, burrowing its way up and out. Loose bits of rock and organic material were caught up in the vortex, strengthening it. When it broke through to the surface, Zephryn focused on expanding it so that it created a space large enough for him to pass through.

Outside the wind became a raging storm, scooping up twigs and leaves as well as small stones. The dust in the air made it almost impossible to see, but Zephryn didn't need to see to know which way to go. Chloe's presence was an invisible beacon.

Da'nat shouted something after him but the roaring wind swept his words away.

You're not going to talk me out of this, Zephryn said, mind to mind.

I do not try. And you would do well not to forget how powerful she is.

I won't. Zephryn hesitated for the briefest of moments. *I'll be back. We both will.*

Yes. And if her mother lives you will need to bring her as well.

Thank you, Da'nat.

May your winds never fail.

The old Ardraci blessing, coming from the Ilezie, was enough to startle Zephryn into almost losing control of his winds. Looking back at the hole leading to the ship he frowned, then used the storm to uproot a tree, toppling it over to conceal the space. He'd figure out how to move it again when the time came.

He moved towards Chloe's house, the storm following in his wake. There were no worries about being seen, the dust and debris churned up in the air was an effective cloak, and he'd already proven at the old mine that any surveillance devices were no match for him. When he was almost there he released the winds, allowing the storm to move off so it could dissipate as it would.

There was no hesitation in him as he entered the house. Chloe's jacket was lying on the floor where she'd dropped it, covered in dust but it appeared to be intact and there was no blood anywhere on it that he could see.

"Chloe?"

He didn't wait for her to answer but continued down the hallway, and suddenly there she was. His arms went around her and he buried his face in her hair, holding her tight. She sobbed out his name and clung to him. He couldn't help himself and started kissing her - her lips, her eyes, her face. They stood that way forever, which wasn't nearly long enough, before he finally loosened his hold.

"Pack your things, your mother's too," he said. "We're getting out of here. All of us."

"Zephryn." She loosened her grip and stood back a pace. "I can't go with you."

A fist clutched at his heart. "Oh, I . . . I just assumed . . ." He backed away a step as well and ran a hand through his hair, dislodging a small cloud of dust and leaves. "I . . . it doesn't matter if you're not feeling what I feel. You can't stay here. It's not safe. You need to leave - we can get your mother the medical attention she needs and then you can go anywhere you want—"

"Oh, Zephryn." Following as he backed away another uncertain step, she wrapped her arms around him again. "You ass. Of course I want to go with you." She choked on her next words. "It's my mother - she's gone."

"Gone?" Zephryn's arms went around her automatically as he looked down at her in shock. "What do you mean she's gone? Gone where?"

"Gannon took her." Chloe's voice was muffled against his shoulder.

He held her as she cried, then picked her up and carried her into her bedroom, sitting down on the bed with her.

"We'll get her back," he promised. "And then Gannon be damned - we're leaving this place. All of us."

* * * * *

152

Da'nat stared after Zephryn. Had he deemed it necessary he could have stopped him, wind or no wind, but it would have served no purpose, other than to expend unnecessary energy and set them against each other. And now events were set in motion and all he could do was wait for the outcome.

He disliked waiting.

How had he let things spin so far out of control? This was supposed to be a simple mission, routine even - follow the energy pulse that had been created when the elemental Pyre released his built-up energy into space, analyze it if possible and calculate its trajectory. Only he'd found it mesmerizing, so much so that he'd tried to touch it with his mind, never for a moment suspecting it was becoming sentient.

It had seen his attempt at contact as a threat, as any lower life form would have, and reacted accordingly. It had lashed out. So in effect, Da'nat was the reason they'd crashed on this world. It was more than that though, he could not help but believe they were here for a reason. This was not a feeling of superstition, but rather one of inevitability.

Things were happening on this world that he was a part of, but had no control over. He disliked feeling like he was being manipulated as much as he disliked waiting, but he wasn't certain what he could do about it.

"I know you're here," Da'nat said after he managed to get the hatch shut again. "Show yourself."

Granny shimmered into view, unsurprised that he knew she was there, and unapologetic.

"It must be exhausting, keeping track of all lives you are trying to control," he said.

"Not control, influence." She spread her hands wide. "Merely nudge them in the right direction."

Da'nat gave a very un-Ilezie like snort of derision. "Do the humans on this world have any idea what you really are?"

"Only one, and he's long gone now."

Cocking his head to one side, he studied her. It was truly amazing, how human she looked. It must take incredible power to maintain such a form.

"There is no one else here," he said. "Why do you not show your true form?"

She lost a little of her arrogance. "I cannot."

The simple statement startled the Ilezie like nothing else could have. "I beg your pardon, I must have misheard."

"I am no longer able to take my original form. I have been in this one too long."

"You underwent the *sh'fused'n*, the merging," he whispered.

"It was necessary at the time," she said briskly.

Obviously she didn't wish to talk about it, but he had to know one thing, "How long?"

"It doesn't matter." She shrugged. "Let me ask *you* something, since we seem to be having a questions and answers session. Why haven't you contacted your home world to tell them what's going on?"

Da'nat had no good answer to give her. Why *hadn't* he tried contacting the home world, or even one of the relay outposts to pass a message along? "How do you know I haven't?" he asked finally.

She leveled a look at him. "Do not fence words with me, youngling," she said. "Show some respect for your elders."

"What do you want with me?" Frustration laced his voice.

"Ah, now that's an easy question to answer. I already have what I wanted from you."

* * * * *

As much as Chloe would have liked to stay in Zephryn's arms, clinging to him like a lifeline, she knew that wasn't possible. At least not right now.

"We need to make plans," she said, resolutely pushing away from him. She swiped an arm across her face to wipe away the last traces of tears and climbed off of his lap. He moved over to give her space to sit beside him, but she got to her feet instead.

"All right," he agreed, watching her pace. "Where do we start?"

"First we talk to Granny. I think she knows more than she's letting on." She stopped with a frown. "Did you see where she went? She was here, talking to me, just before you arrived."

Zephryn got to his feet as well. "I have a few questions of my own to ask her. Like what she hit me with."

"She hit you?" Granny said she'd knocked him out, but she assumed she'd given him a drugged beverage or something along those lines. The idea was almost ludicrous, a tiny old woman knocking him unconscious.

"All I know is that she was behind me when I tried to leave to go to the mine, and the next thing I know I was back aboard my ship, waking up with one hell of a headache."

Chloe sat back down on the bed. "This just keeps getting more and more impossible. How did she get you to your ship without being seen? And how did she get you back on board, for that matter, the ship is buried. Or at least it was."

"It still is," he assured her. "As for how she got me back on board . . ." Here he hesitated. "She may have had help."

"Help? What kind of help?"

"Chloe . . ." He sat back down beside her, taking one of her hands in his. "There's something I need to tell you. I should have told you from the beginning, but there were reasons to keep it secret. And then things started happening and I didn't know how to tell you, and now . . . well, you need to know the truth."

She place her free hand over his to reassure him. He seemed so nervous."Zephryn, whatever it is, you can tell me."

"I wasn't alone on the ship."

Chapter Twenty-two

Zephryn could feel Chloe's withdrawal, even before she tried to take her hands back. He quickly brought his other hand around, sandwiching hers between his.

"It's not what you think," he told her. "His name is Da'nat and he's part watchdog, part partner, and we're working on being friends. He's an Ilezie, and on Ardraci it's considered quite an honour when an Ilezie attaches themselves to you and they're not like us and they're a little secretive and. . ." He realized he was babbling and tried to stem the flow of words. "I'm sorry."

"Why didn't you tell me about him before?"

He took it as a good sign that she left her hands where they were. "He asked me not to, when I first woke up here. It wasn't an unusual request coming from him, the Ilezie really don't like interacting with any non-Ardraci, and I didn't think we were going to be here that long. Then later . . . well, things started happening and I just never got the chance."

She nodded, but he wasn't reassured.

"Say something," he asked.

Chloe gave him a searching glance. "Is there anything else you're keeping from me?"

"No."

"This . . . Da'nat, you said his name was?"

Zephryn nodded.

"Will he help get my mother back?"

"I don't know," he said honestly. "He didn't stop me from coming back to you, and he told me to bring both you and your mother back to the ship. But I don't know if he can do more than that. Like I said, the Ilezie aren't like us."

It was her turn to nod. "Is it safe to assume that he made any repairs necessary to your ship?"

"I . . ." To his chagrin, Zephryn realized he never thought to check. He reached out with his mind.

Da'nat? Are you there?

I am here.

There was something odd about the voice in his head. If Zephryn didn't know better, he'd say the Ilezie sounded stressed. *Is everything all right?*

Do not concern yourself with me. You must focus on the task at hand. I cannot help you in what you must do.

I kind of figured that. But what about the ship? How badly is it damage, will we be able to take off again?

I was able to make the necessary repairs, Da'nat said. *The ship is fully functional.*

Okay. Great. Look, there's a slight problem—

Tierra is missing.

Somehow Zephryn wasn't surprised Da'nat already knew this. *Can you tell me where she is?*

There was a slight pause before Da'nat answered. *I regret, I cannot.*

We have to find her.

I understand.

We'll be there as soon as we can, Zephryn told him. *Just have the ship ready.*

I'll be waiting.

The conversation had only taken a moment or two, but when Zephryn came back to himself it was to find Chloe staring at him with a concerned look on her face.

"What?"

"Where did you go?" she asked.

He flushed slightly. "Sorry. I was speaking to Da'nat, mind to mind."

"Mind to mind?"

"Yes, it's . . . it's hard to explain. Normally he's the one that initiates contact, but if I focus I can send my thoughts to him. I was asking him about the ship." As explanations he thought it fell a little short, but she seemed to accept it.

"Oh. And is the ship in working order?"

"Yes, we're good to go."

She hesitated a second, then asked, "Can . . . can he help us get my mother back?"

"I'm sorry, no."

When she withdrew her hands from between his, he felt a keen sense of loss, as though she was pulling away. "The first thing we need to figure out is where Gannon would be holding her."

"The infirmary would be too obvious a choice," Chloe said. "I don't—"

There was a sharp rapping at the front door. She paled and clutched at his arm. "I have to get that."

"I know. I'll be right here. If there's the slightest danger . . ."

She made a poor attempt at a reassuring smile. "I'll yell for you to use your wind to push them outside again."

When he looked at her in surprise, she gave a short laugh. "Once they're outside I can open the ground up under them."

The rapping noise was repeated, a little more forcefully. Chloe gave his arm a squeeze and then got up to see who it was. Zephryn got up as well, stationing himself by the door so he could listen in case there was trouble.

Chloe wasn't gone long. When she came back she was wearing a puzzled frown and holding a white paper, folded and sealed.

"It was just a miner delivering this," she said, waving the paper.

"What is it?"

She broke open the seal, frown deepening as she read what was written on it. Without saying a word, she handed it to Zephryn.

It was from Gannon, an invitation to dinner to discuss the terms of her mother's release.

* * * * *

Zephryn looked up from the note in his hand, taking in her slumped shoulders and the lines of fatigue on her face.

"Look," he said. "This dinner is hours away. Why don't you get cleaned up while I fix us something to eat, then you should have a rest for a while."

"I would like to get cleaned up," she admitted. "But I don't think I could eat anything." There was a gurgling noise from her mid-section and she flushed. "Well, maybe just a bite or two."

He chuckled, though he felt anything but lighthearted, and hugged her to him, then gave her a gentle push towards the bathroom. Catching sight of himself in the mirror above her dresser, he grimaced at the dust and dirt left on him from the wind and cleaned up as best he could in the kitchen sink. It would have to do.

By the time Chloe reappeared, he had a light salad cobbled together from vegetables that Granny had brought from her garden, and a piece of fish he'd found in the ice box simmering in a creamy sauce. Her eyes lit up when she saw the food.

"It looks good enough to eat," she told him.

"That's the idea."

After a few bites she hummed with pleasure. "You're spoiling me - I could get used to this."

"Good," he said. "I think you need a little spoiling."

"Zephryn, I—"

"No," he shook his head. "No serious talk. Serious can come later. Let's just enjoy our meal and then you get some rest."

"But—"

"We'll talk, I promise. But later."

"Fine," she said with a sigh, then deliberately changed the subject. "Tell me about Ardraci."

"I wasn't there long, you understand, but what I saw of it was beautiful. It was . . . "He looked away as he thought about it for a moment. "If you took a colony of artists and let them design a world, I don't think they'd be able to come up with anything more breath-taking. The buildings are tall spires or rounded domes, which shouldn't work well together but somehow do. There are gardens everywhere, with waterfalls and fountains. There's little industry so the air is fresh and pure."

"It sounds like a paradise."

"It is," he said, looking back at her with a self-depreciating grin. "Which is why it was so hard for those of us raised in the compound to adapt easily to it. Our world was grey and sterile and suddenly there's this explosion of colour and space."

"It must have presented quite the challenge."

His grin broadened. "The earth elementals are the ones who adapted the easiest."

She laughed. "But of course!" Shaking her head, she said. "I must confess I find it difficult to think of myself as an elemental," she stumbled over the word. "I'm still just a miner, albeit a miner with an unusual gift." Her statement was punctuated with a yawn.

"A tired miner with an unusual gift," he said, laughing along with her. "Go get some rest. I'll clean this up."

Nodding, Chloe rose from the table. She took two steps towards her bedroom and then turned.

"Zephryn?"

He looked up from the act of gathering up the plates.

"Could you come with me?" She looked almost embarrassed as she added, "I . . . I don't want to be alone."

Seeing the look of vulnerability on her face, there was no way he could refuse. "Now that you mention it, I think I could use a rest too."

Leaving the dishes, he was by her side in two strides and took her hand. Kissing her knuckles he took charge, leading her to the bedroom. There was just barely enough room for them both on her bed. He lay with his back to the wall and held her back to his front, one arm across her waist to hold her in place.

"This is nice," she said sleepily.

"I could get used to this," he whispered, kissing the top of her head.

There was no reply as her breathing evened out and she slept. Zephryn thought nothing had ever felt so right as he held her in his arms, and at last he, too, slept.

Chapter Twenty-three

Something was tickling Zephryn's nose. He frowned, eyes still closed, and swatted at it.

There was a soft giggle, and the tickling sensation returned. His eyes snapped open. He must have been more tired than he realized, to have slept so soundly. Chloe was leaning over him, tickling his nose with her hair. She was straddling him as he lay on his back . . . and she was naked.

"What's going on?" he croaked.

"What do you think's going on?" she asked with a mischievous smile.

"I think I'm dreaming a most wonderful dream. Either that or you've decided to kill me in the most pleasurable way possible."

She leaned down further to kiss him, the fine silk of her hair sliding across his face. By this time he was fully awake, but when he reached for her she sat back up out of his reach.

"No," she said, shaking her head.

"No? But—"

Laughing at his expression, she gave him another quick kiss

and started on the fastenings to his shirt. "What I mean is, you're not allowed to touch. This is all about me, so I'm going to do all the work. Keep your hands to yourself."

"If it's all about you, shouldn't I be the one doing all the work?" he asked hopefully.

"The work is half the fun," she said, scooting down just enough for him to sit up so she could remove his shirt.

He smothered a groan as she moved down further to start to work on his pants, his fists clenching the blanket beneath him to keep from reaching for her.

"You're taking an unconscionably long time about this. Are you sure you don't want my help?"

She stopped what she was doing, a patently fake look of concern on her face. "If you'd rather we didn't . . ."

"No! I mean, don't stop. I mean—" His breath left him in a whoosh as she ran a finger from the base of his throat down the center of his chest. Zephryn's eyes narrowed. She wanted to play, did she?

The breeze was so subtle that at first she didn't notice it. It swept over her skin, a ghostly touch, just cool enough to make her nipples pucker. It moved in a serpentine pattern, across her belly, up and around each breast in turn. Chloe shivered and looked down at Zephryn accusingly.

"What are you doing?"

"Me?" He strove for an innocent expression. "I'm keeping my hands to myself, just as you requested."

"Zephryn, you—" Her accusation ended in an outrush of breath as she felt a ghostly caress over her most intimate places. Chloe moaned in pleasure as she arched her back, forgetting she was supposed to be the one in charge.

Zephryn's wind seemed to be everywhere at once, cooling her heated flesh and at the same time making her burn with desire. Pleasure coiled deep in her belly, winding tighter and tighter like a spring until all at once it broke, and she shuddered to a climax, calling out his name.

She was still shuddering with the aftershocks when she collapsed on his chest.

"You cheated," she accused, gasping for breath.

"Yes, I did," he admitted.

While she was still weak from the after effects he deftly rolled them over so she was underneath him and quickly finished divesting himself of his clothing.

"That was . . . amazing."

"I know." He grinned down at her, then slowly lowered his head to kiss her - a lingering kiss on the lips and then a trail of kisses along her jaw and down her throat. He could feel her pulse in the side of her neck beating rapidly still, and continued down the slope of her breast, drawing one taut peak into his mouth.

Chloe moaned, threading her hands through his hair as he lavished attention on first one breast, then the other. Her back arched as he bite her lightly.

"Zephryn!" His name came out as a gasp.

"You have the most perfect breasts . . ." He raised his head to look at her; she'd never looked more beautiful, her face flushed with desire, her hair tousled, her eyes ever so slightly glazed.

"I can't wait. Please," she begged.

One last kiss to the tip of each breast and he moved upwards again. His head dipped down to kiss her lips once more, swallowing her gasp as he slid home. She wrapped her legs around his waist as he stroked in and out, but he kept his pace unhurried, drawing out the pleasure for both of them.

She trembled beneath him, covered in a fine sheen of sweat. He made love to her as if it was the last time they'd be together - for all they knew it might be. But as much as he tried to make it last, their being together was still too new. All too soon his pace quickened, his strokes harder and faster.

"Yes," she gasped.

Somehow he managed to hang on until she tightened around him, crying out his name, and then he let the pleasure wash over him as well. Zephryn slowed, then stopped. Wrapping his arms around her, he shifted so that he wasn't crushing her while they caught their breath.

"I still say you cheated," Chloe said, when she could speak again.

Her head rested on his chest as his laughter rumbled under her ear.

* * * * *

Chloe stood looking down at Zephryn as he slept. She knew she'd taken him by surprise earlier, but she wanted a memory of something good, something hers, to take with her to her confrontation with Gannon. And Zephryn was the best thing that had happened to her in her life.

Fully dressed, she was putting off leaving for her appointment until the last possible second, and that second was now. She'd thought long and hard about what to wear for this meeting with Gannon, and although the invitation had been for dinner, she dressed in a clean mine uniform.

It was tempting to wake Zephryn up, but she decided leaving him would be worse if he was awake. He would look at her with those storm-filled grey eyes of his and something inside her would whither at the thought of having to say goodbye. No, this was better. Sneaking away like a thief in the night.

Resisting the urge to give him one last kiss goodbye, she gave him a lingering glance instead and then resolutely left him behind, leaving the house and shutting the door firmly behind her. If there were tears pricking at her eyes as she started down the path towards the mine offices, she put it down to the dust churned up by the light breeze.

It took her a moment to realize it, but there was something odd about the puff of air. The leaves on the trees around her were still, but the air circled around her, lifting her hair, plucking at her clothing. Suddenly she smiled. Zephryn! She hadn't fooled him at all, leaving as she had.

"I'm sorry," she whispered.

The wind caressed her cheek, almost as if he could understand her words.

Her good mood lasted until she reached the mine office. Her stomach sank to the vicinity of her boots as she realized all the support staff had gone for the night. Her steps slowed. The breeze that had been following her caressed the back of her neck, giving her courage. It was good to know she wasn't alone, even if there was little Zephryn could do to help.

Chloe stiffened her spine and knocked sharply on the door to Gannon's office, then opened the door when she heard him say, "Come."

"Very punctual," he told her. "I like that in a woman."

"What have you done with my mother?"

"Not yet." He waggled a finger at her. "My instructions were that we discuss this over dinner." He waved towards the round table set up in the corner of his office.

She was both surprised and a little relieved to see it set up for three.

"I believe you've met my newest mining assistant," Gannon said.

Chloe hadn't noticed the man lurking in the shadows and when he came forward she gave a start of surprise. "You!"

"Surprised to see me?" Ulrik smirked at her.

"What's he doing here?" she demanded.

"Sit," Gannon ordered. "We can talk while we eat."

He seated himself at the table and after a moment's hesitation, Chloe joined him. Ulrik served them from a series of covered dishes that had been set up on a wheeled cart.

"I told you you'd pay for what you did," he whispered as he served Chloe.

"I'm disappointed in you Chloe," Gannon said. "You've been holding out on me."

"How so?" she asked, ignoring the food steaming on her plate.

"My new friend Ulrik tells me you're far more powerful than you've been letting on."

She glanced at Ulrik and then back towards Gannon. "And what would he know about it?"

"I know about the Elementals, and what they can do. I was a miner on Anchyre when an Elemental brought the world back to life. It shut down the mines there."

"Really? But what's that got to do with me?"

"I saw you," he hissed. "In the old mine. You and that man. I saw the things you could do."

Chloe paled. She should have listened to Zephryn, he was sure there'd been someone watching them. A cool breeze washed over her, calming her. He was still with her. How was he able to do that?

"Yes," Gannon broke in. "That man you were with in the old mine . . . Who was he? Was he the pilot of the ship?"

"How could there be a pilot when we never found a ship?" she countered.

"Mark my words. I *will* find out who he is."

Chloe dabbed at her mouth with her napkin and carefully placed her knife and fork onto her plate. "This meal is over. Now where is my mother?"

Gannon eyed her a moment, then nodded. "Very well. Follow me."

He pushed back from the table and she followed suit. Ulrik remained seated and helped himself to another glass of wine.

Chloe walked behind Gannon as he led her from the office and down the hall. He stopped in front of a metal door and punched in a numbered code. There was an audible click, then he opened the door and gestured for Chloe to precede him.

Her mother lay in what looked like a glass coffin. There were wires leading into it and it was lit from within. A control panel on the side held a series of buttons and flashing lights.

"What have you done?" she whispered.

Chapter Twenty-four

Zephryn frowned as he sat cross-legged on Chloe's bed. It took a tremendous amount of concentration to follow Chloe with his wind. Short of following her and risk getting caught, it was the only way he could think of to discover where they were holding her mother.

His plan was simple. Find out where Gannon was keeping Tierra and go in and rescue her, taking her to the ship. After that there'd be nothing on this world that would stop him from taking Chloe away from this place.

It was a strange sensation, using his wind in this manner. He couldn't see with it, of course, but he could get a sense of time and place. Chloe's emotions were easy to monitor, and when there was a spike - he didn't know if it was fear or anger - he tried to project calm through his link.

As he'd hoped, Gannon showed her where he was keeping her mother. He couldn't explain how he knew, he just did. And more, he was positive he could find the place again with his wind. On impulse he had the breeze caress Chloe's face, hoping to ease her distress. Soon this would be over.

A noise from outside of the room distracted him enough that he lost his hold on his wind and the link was lost. Zephryn scowled. "By the winds!"

Uncoiling himself, he stood and stretched. He hadn't realized how long he'd been sitting there, his muscles were stiff. The noise came again; it sounded like a chair being moved in the kitchen. With a sigh he went to investigate. It was probably nothing more than Granny poking about and he wondered was she was up to this time.

"Granny, I think you should know—" He broke off what he was going to say. Looking around the kitchen he could see no trace of the old woman. "Granny?"

The door to Tierra's room was still open and he glanced inside. Nothing. Shrugging, he turned and padded back down the hall to the front sitting room. "Granny? What kind of game are you playing now?"

Once again he found the room empty. Zephryn frowned. If it wasn't Granny that made the noise, then what?

A whisper of movement behind him was all the warning he got. There was a burst of pain in the back of his head, then darkness.

* * * * *

"And just where do you think you might be going," Granny asked from behind.

Da'nat gave a start, and turned. He'd been peering out through the open hatch, gauging the obstacles blocking the way out. Though he was capable of teleporting himself, that didn't always mean he should. And he had a feeling he'd need to conserve his energy.

"Zephryn is in trouble. I can feel it. I'm going to help."

The old woman was already shaking her head. "That ain't such a good idea. He—"

"Stop talking like you're some dotty old woman," Da'nat said angrily. "If you're not going to appear as you truly are, then at least speak like it!"

"Very well." She drew herself up proudly. "You must let things play out as they will."

Da'nat drew in a breath to protest but she continued. "If that means injury to your charge, then I am sorry for it. But he is not what is important here. Only the girl is."

"Of course *you* would say that. Have you grown so old that you do not remember what it is like to guide one of the Ardraci?"

"Are you so young that you do not fully understand why we created the Ardraci in the first place?" she countered.

His eyes widened. "We did not create them. They were always there, just as we were."

"Then why do we involve ourselves in their lives?"

"We take care of them, guide them. Nothing more."

"And the testing we put them through?"

"The testing is to help teach them control."

"Can you really be so naive?" she said in a voice of wonder.

Shaking her head, she motioned for him to follow her to the ship's lounge. They sat in opposite chairs and Da'nat waited for her to speak. The sense of foreboding he felt regarding Zephryn increased ten-fold.

"What happened to you?" he asked suddenly. "How did the great Gra'anna become more . . ."

"Human than Ilezie?" she asked wryly. She sighed. "It is a long story. But after centuries of travel I finally came to a time of ascension where I was too far from the home world. My body was failing. For a time I moved from *illarie* to *illarie*, but vessels are rare to begin with and they became even fewer and harder to find. Finally, there were none."

"I did not realize a non-Ardraci could become an *illarie*."

She shrugged. "Only one in ten thousand can. The woman whose body this is was a friend. When she lost her husband she wished to end her own existence. I offered her a better solution, the *torngarmi*."

Da'nat's eyes widened in shock. While he knew of the *torngarmi*, the total merging, it was rarely performed between two Ilezie, and for it to involve an Ilezie and an Ardraci was all but unheard of. But for it to have been performed between an Ilezie and a human - it was impossible!

* * * * *

Chloe could no longer feel Zephryn's wind as she followed Gannon back to his office. She hoped that meant he'd marked the location of her mother and even now was coming up with a plan to rescue her. She needed to stall for time.

As they entered the room the communicator on Gannon's wrist went off. "Yes? . . . What do you mean he's gone?"

He listened for a moment, expression growing grim as he glanced towards Chloe and then away. He paced over to the other side of the office to finish the conversation. His words were clipped and sharp, but he was too far away for Chloe to hear what he was saying. When he was done he tossed the communicator onto his desk before seating himself at the table.

The table had been cleared and a map spread out over the top. Chloe's eyes flicked towards Ulrik, who was standing off to the side, before taking the seat Gannon indicated.

"All right, Gannon," she said when she got tired of him staring at her in silence. "What exactly do you want?"

"Tell me something," he said as Ulrik poured him a drink like he was some kind of waiter. "Those tremors we've been experiencing lately, are you responsible for them?"

She hesitated a moment. "Possibly." When he would have responded she held up a hand and continued, "I'm not trying to be evasive, I truly don't know for sure. My power lies more with growing things than causing earth tremors."

"She lies!" Ulrik spoke up. He moved around so he was facing her. "I saw you and your lover going into the old mine. You can somehow sense the metals in the ore and draw them to you."

"I was able to extract a small amount of gold," she countered. "And did you not see how the effort made me weak?"

"You made the earth move beneath you."

"A small upheaval!"

"You held the earth back when the mine collapsed," Ulrik hissed. "Then you were able to dig your way out."

"You! You set off the explosion! You tried to kill us!" She glared at him.

"Enough!" Gannon set his glass down with a thump."I already know of your ability to sense the different ores, but is it true you have the ability to draw the ore to you instead of digging for it? Do not forget I can pull the plug on your mother's life support if I suspect you're lying."

It seemed a harmless enough gift to admit to. "Yes."

"Your ability to grow weeds does not interest me, but can you move through the earth, as Ulrik has told me?"

Here's where it became tricky. So far Gannon didn't seem

particularly interested in the man she was with in the cavern, but she had no doubt that would change if he suspected Zephryn was gifted as well. Their survival of the cave-in had been a joint effort.

"I was lucky," she said at last. "The earth was very loose and it was only a short length of the passage that was blocked."

Ulrik stirred angrily but Gannon cut him off with a gesture. He stared thoughtfully at Chloe. "And the tremors?" he asked again.

"I didn't mean to cause them," she said. "They were involuntary." She shrugged. "I was tired and worried about my mother, my control slipped."

Once again Ulrik looked like he wanted to say something. She flicked him a glance and said, "Yes, in the old mine I was able to raise the earth slightly, but it was only a few inches and it took a lot of concentration. I think a lot of the tremors we've been experiencing are naturally occurring."

Gannon took a sip of his drink, staring at her the whole time. Chloe tried not to fidget under his gaze. She wished she knew what he was thinking.

"So now you know the full extent of my abilities," she said when she could stand his silence no longer. "Are you going to release my mother?"

"All in good time," he said. "I think we need a small test of your abilities."

"You mean causing the cave-in that trapped me and my crew wasn't enough?" she snapped. "We could have been killed, in fact one of us was."

He waved a dismissive hand. "It was a chance I was willing to take, especially in the face of the potential rewards."

The arrogance of the man! Chloe clamped her mouth shut so she wouldn't say anything she'd regret.

"Yes, a test," he said thoughtfully.

A knot began to form in the pit of her stomach.

"I want you to put the Lightning Strike out of business."

"What?" The Lightning Strike was the smallest of the five mining territories. It was also the closest one to them. Generally it was left alone because it was so small.

"I want you to see to it that Lightning Strike is closed down."

"And how am I supposed to do that?" The very idea made her sick to her stomach. All those people out of work? It was unthinkable.

"Collapse the mine, seal up the tunnels, move all the potential sources for profit too deep for them to get to - I don't care how you do it as long as you do."

"No, it's too dangerous; people will be hurt, maybe even killed!"

"I don't care how you do it, but you have twenty-four hours to see that it's done." He spread his hands wide. "Otherwise, there just might be a power outage to your mother's life pod."

Chapter Twenty-five

Zephryn woke with a groan. The back of his head hurt, and when he reached back there he felt cloth. Someone had knocked him out, but then bandaged him up. It didn't make sense.

"He's awake," a voice said.

"All right," a second voice said. "You boys best get out of here now, I can handle things from here. But thanks for your help."

There were the sounds of more than one other person moving around, a few murmurs Zephryn couldn't quite make out, and then silence again. He opened his eyes, blinking several times to adjust to the light.

"Easy there son," the second voice said. Someone came over to help as he tried to sit up. "Didn't mean to hit you so hard."

"Why'd you hit me in the first place?" Zephryn asked, wincing at the sound of his own voice. He swung his legs over the side of the cot he'd been lying on and waited for the room to stop spinning.

"Here, drink this," the man with him said, handing him a cup. "It'll make you feel better."

"And I should trust you why?"

"Because I'm here to help. Granny sent me."

Zephryn took the cup from him, gave the contents a dubious sniff, and then drank it down. "Who are you?" he asked. "And where am I?"

"My name's Martin," the man said, taking the empty cup from him and setting it aside. "I'm—"

"Chloe's crew chief," Zephryn said. "Mind telling me what's going on Martin?"

"Damned if I know, son," Martin said with a sigh. He sat down in a nearby chair.

Zephryn looked around curiously. It looked like they were in a cave of some sort - hard packed dirt floor, the walls shored up with timber, but with the odd root poking through here and there. The light came from a pair of matching battery powered lamps set into the wall. "Where am I?"

"This is a cave Tierra, Chloe's mother, created. Not sure why. I guess it was some place she could escape to if the need arose."

"So why are we here?"

Martin ran a grimy hand through his short, grey-streaked hair. "Granny came to me, wanting a favour. We all have a healthy respect for that woman and her wanting a favour isn't something anyone around here would take lightly. She said she needed me to bring you here, that there would be terrible danger to Chloe if I didn't."

"Chloe!" How could he have forgotten what she was doing? "Where is she? I have to—"

"Now just hold on, son," Martin said, waving him back down when he would have risen. "She's not here. As far as I know she's still in her meeting with Gannon."

"You know about that?"

Martin nodded. "Granny told me. And I can't say as I like it one bit. There's just too many strange things going on around here."

"Don't I know it," Zephryn muttered. "Maybe you should start at the beginning," he said, sitting back with a sigh.

"Granny came to me and told me that Gannon found out the truth about Chloe's ability to manipulate the earth —"

"You know?"

"I've known Chloe since she was a little girl, of course I know."

"But Gannon didn't know the full extent of her abilities, how did he find out?"

"No idea. All I know is Gannon sent his men to take Tierra and was coming back for you. Now you I didn't know about. Course I knew someone put a smile on that girl's face, but Chloe hiding a stranger in her own home?" He shook his head in disbelief.

Zephryn didn't know what to say.

"Where'd you come from, anyway?"

"My ship crashed on this world." Zephryn spread his hands wide. "Chloe found me and took me back to her house - she hid me from Gannon. I've been hiding there ever since."

"Well I'll be damned." A wide grin split Martin's face. "I always figured that girl had spunk. And right under Gannon's nose, too."

Zephryn couldn't help grinning back. He was feeling a little proud of her himself. "So now what, Martin?"

The other man sobered up and sighed. "Granny just said it

was important to get to you before Gannon's men. Sorry about that, by the way. They were nipping at my heels and I didn't have time to argue with you. I might have hit you just a tad harder than I intended."

Rubbing the back of his head, Zephryn's smile turned rueful. "No harm done," he said. "All in a good cause, I guess. Wait a minute." He sat up straight. "You said Gannon was sending men back for me after he'd taken Tierra?"

"That's what Granny told me."

"How did he find out about me, and where I was staying?"

For that, Martin had no answer.

* * * * *

Chloe felt a chill that went deeper than the temperature around her or the task that had been set before her. She had arrived back at her home and Zephryn was not waiting for her. In fact, there was no sign he had ever been here at all - there were no extra dishes left out, the bed was made, even his uniform was gone. Had he gone back to his ship without telling her?

She waited for the hurt that that thought should bring, but it never came. He wouldn't do that to her, she knew it in her gut. There was too much between them now for her not to trust him. Something else was going on, she just had to figure out what it was.

But now, more than ever, she needed him. She need his warmth and reassurance. She needed his arms around her and his voice whispering in her ear, telling her everything was going to work out. That he'd take her away from this place and she'd never have to work in a mine again, unless it was by her choice.

She sat on the bed they'd shared and stroked the blanket. What could have happened to him? A single tear traced down her cheek. Chloe had never felt so alone in all her life.

"I'm sorry, I meant to be here before you returned."

Somehow she wasn't at all surprised to hear Granny's voice. She turned her head and looked at her mutely.

"Oh, don't look at me like that. I didn't do anything to him this time. Well, not directly anyway."

Still, Chloe didn't say anything. She was feeling too defeated for words.

"Gannon found out about him," Granny said, a frown furrowing her brow at Chloe's lack of response. "He was sending his men for him so I had to move him fast."

"What did you do?"

"I had Martin take him to the old cave of your mother's."

She thought about that for a moment, how his comforting wind had abruptly disappeared. "I doubt it was that easy."

"Well, no. There weren't no time to reason with the boy so Martin had to knock him out."

Chloe got to her feet. "I need to see him."

Granny was already shaking her head. "It's too dangerous. You'd be leading Gannon straight to him and then where would you be? He'd have two hostages against you instead of just one."

Slowly Chloe sat down again. Her eyes filled with tears. "What am I supposed to do?"

With a sigh Granny sat down beside her and put a comforting arm around her shoulders. "You do what you have to. It's all any of us can do."

"You don't understand. Gannon wants —" there was a hitch

in her breath and she continued. "He wants me to use my gift to destroy the Lightning Strike mine. I can't do it! All those people, someone's bound to get hurt. I couldn't live with myself."

"Shush now," Granny said. "Just think for a minute. All you need to do is make sure nobody's in the mine when you shut it down. Now how would you do that?"

Chloe sniffled and considered Granny's question. "I'd sound the alarm to evacuate the mine."

"You ain't gonna get anywhere near the Lightning Strike's alarms. You need to think of some way to make sure someone else sounds the alarm."

"A mine collapse," Chloe said. She swiped a hand across her face, wiping away the tears. "No, that's still too dangerous. Someone could get hurt." She pulled away from Granny. "I know, gas! If anyone were to detect any sign of gas they'd evacuate the mine and keep everyone out until it was thoroughly investigated."

Without even thinking twice about it, she closed her eyes and sent her awareness deep into the earth towards the Lightning Strike mine. "Yes," she said. "That could work. There are several pockets of gas near where they're working. The gas itself is inert, but they wouldn't know that until they do a thorough analysis."

"Wait!" Granny grasped her arm and gave it a shake. "Not yet."

Opening her eyes again, Chloe looked at her. "Why not? The sooner I get this done, the sooner I get my mother back and Zephryn can take us away!" She hadn't realized her voice was rising and made an effort to calm herself.

Granny looked at her pityingly. "Do you really think

Gannon'll stop with the Lightning Strike?"

Chloe wilted under the old woman's steady gaze. "No, I don't suppose he will. Not as long as he has my mother."

"We'll get her back, there's no doubt about that. But it'll take time. In the meantime, right now Gannon's only guessing at a lot of what you can do," Granny told her. "And he has no idea of the range you have."

"You're right," Chloe said slowly. "As far as I know, I'm not even limited to distance. If Gannon ever found that out, who knows what he'd have me do, or who he'd target next." She shuddered at the thought.

Granny remained silent, letting her work it out for herself.

"Lightning Strike is miles from here." Chloe sat back and considered her options. "If Gannon thought my range was limited . . ." She stood up and headed towards the seldom used com-unit. "I have an idea."

Chapter Twenty-six

Chloe stood hesitating in front of the com unit, her thoughts chaotic. Though she didn't say anything, she had to wonder how Granny had known Gannon's men had been coming for Zephryn. Part of her thought there was a lot more going on that she was privy to. Granny had been acting so oddly lately, could she even trust her anymore?

She punched in the call signal for Gannon's office. She was going to have to at least trust Granny to keep Zephryn safe for the moment.

"You have twenty-one hours left," Gannon told her.

"Despite what you may think you know of me," Chloe told him with more bravado than she was feeling, "my range is limited. I'll need to be closer to the Lightning Strike before I can shut it down."

He frowned into the viewer. "You shouldn't have to be that close to create one of your earth tremors."

"I will if I want to direct it to the right place," she snapped. "I've never done something on this scale before. The closer I am, the better chance I have of hitting my target."

Gannon drummed his fingers on his desk while he considered what she said. He turned the sound off on the com unit and consulted someone she couldn't see. Probably Ulrik. Turning the sound back on, he said, "All right. I'll send a hover-car for you. Be ready in half an hour."

Without further another word, he broke contact.

Chloe let out a deep breath and turned to Granny. "You need to get a hold of Martin," she said firmly. "There's not going to be a better time to rescue my mother than while Gannon's attention is focused on what I'm doing."

"I agree," Granny said, looking a little surprised.

A little surprised herself at her new found determination, Chloe continued. "Lightning Strike is about forty-five minutes away by hover-car, so Zephryn and Martin will have that long to get into position."

Chloe went back to the bed and sat cross-legged on it.

"What are you doing?" Granny asked.

"Whoever takes me to the mine is going to be watching me like a hawk - Gannon will expect me to collapse the mine as soon as I get there. I'm going to bring the gas to the surface now, to give them time to evacuate."

Closing her eyes, she sent her awareness into the earth and westward. She couldn't just create the gas, so she had seek out the naturally occurring pockets of it and coax it to the surface. The thought crossed her mind, would that be something Zephryn might have been able to do for her, create noxious gases?

Creating a series of minute fractures and fissures, she guided the gas to where she wanted it to go. Too slow. Giving it a pathway was not enough; she needed the gas to move quicker. Utilizing the control Zephryn had taught her, she contracted the earth creating the pockets, forcing the gas upwards.

"There," she said with satisfaction. "That should do it."

There was a pounding on her front door and her eyes snapped open. She'd been so caught up in what she was doing she'd been unaware of the passing time. It was no surprise that Granny had once more disappeared. As soon as her mother was safe she needed to have a long talk with that old woman.

The knock on her door repeated and she hurried to answer it. Ulrik smirked at her.

"Your stalling tactics won't work with me. Let's go."

He reached for her arm but she jerked it away. "Don't touch me!" she hissed.

"You'd do well to start being nicer to me. I'm Gannon's right hand man now, and he listens to what I say."

"Good for him. I don't."

Chloe got into the hover car beside the driver, leaving Ulrik to crawl into the back. She wasn't overly worried about him - he wouldn't dare to try anything in front of a witness. She'd just have to make sure he didn't catch her alone.

They didn't talk on their way to Lightning Strike. Chloe watched the scenery speeding past, while the driver - she thought his name was Kefton, one of Gannon's flunkies - focused on his driving.

"Not too close," Ulrik ordered. "We don't want anyone from Lightning Strike to spot us."

Kefton glanced at Chloe for confirmation. Clearly he was not pleased to be taking orders from Ulrik.

"If you can get us about a mile from the mine, that would be perfect," she told him.

He did as she asked while Ulrik fumed in the back seat. Once they were parked, Chloe left the vehicle.

"Stay here," she told the two men when they would have followed. "I have to do this alone."

"Gannon said—"

"I don't care what Gannon said," she told Ulrik. "If you break my concentration at the wrong time there's no telling what could happen. Would you like to be the one telling him that it's your fault I messed up?"

"Fine, just don't go too far," he ordered.

Chloe wished at that moment she'd been blessed with Zephryn's gift. She'd have smacked that superior look right off Ulrik's face with a blast of wind. Instead she had to content herself with just ignoring him and moving several yards away from the vehicle.

She knew every move she made would reported back to Gannon so she needed to make this look good. Kneeling down, she placed her palms flat on the ground. On a whim she had the plants around her bloom, just for effect. A fleeting smile crossed her face as she heard a gasp behind her.

The gas had done its work, she was fairly certain the mines were cleared of workers. Hopefully there hadn't been enough time for a team to suit up and be sent in to investigate. Opening herself up to her gift, she searched out the faults under the mine. There weren't many of them so she was forced to create her own.

It wasn't easy. The ground deep under the Lightning Strike was solid bedrock, making it the safest of all the mines. She was forced to go deeper, which made the land underneath them unstable as well. Ignoring the tremors she focused on the mine itself, caving in tunnel after tunnel. They could hear the roar of the collapse from where they were parked, and seconds later the cave-in siren.

Keeping Granny's advice in mind, Chloe sagged where she sat, feigning a tiredness she did not feel. If Gannon believed collapsing a small mine like this one had her on the brink of exhaustion, perhaps he would not think she was as useful as he hoped.

* * * * *

"How much longer are we supposed to wait here?" Zephryn demanded. He *needed* to be with Chloe. This waiting around was driving him crazy. As much as he didn't want to hurt Martin, he knew the man was something of a father-figure to Chloe, he didn't think he was going to be able to stay underground much longer.

"Granny said she'd come for us when it was safe," Martin told him, his voice betraying his exasperation. This was not the first time Zephryn had asked that.

"Granny!" he ground out. Spinning on his heel, he began pacing back and forth, as he had been for the last hour. He had a thing or two he wanted to say to that old woman, once he got his hands on her. There was a lot more to her than met the eye.

Fists clenched, he turned and paced back again.

Martin watched him for a few more minutes and then suddenly asked, "You're claustrophobic, aren't you?"

"Slightly," he admitted, not stopping his pacing.

"No wonder you're so antsy. Here," he held out a flask. "Take a swig of this, it might help."

Zephryn's steps faltered. He stopped beside Martin and opened his mouth to refuse, then shrugged and accepted the flask. Taking a large gulp, he handed the flask back and started coughing, eyes tearing up.

"What was in that?" he asked, voice raspy.

Martin grinned. "Just a little something me and the boys cook up in one of the storage sheds." He took a drink himself. "This is one of the smoothest batches yet." He held the flask out to Zephryn again.

Zephryn hesitated only a moment before helping himself to another drink. It went down a little easier this time, probably because his taste buds had been burned away by the first drink. Shaking his head, he said, "I'm pretty sure that's the same stuff used to fuel my ship."

Martin just chuckled.

"I can't stay here much longer," Zephryn admitted.

"Well that's a good thing, 'cause you're coming with us," a new voice said.

They turned to see three men holding laser rifles pointed in their direction. Zephryn hesitated using his wind - despite everything, he didn't want Martin hurt. He was unfamiliar with weapons and was uncertain how his wind would affect them. That slight hesitation was all they needed. The leader of the trio nodded his head and the man on the far right brought up a smaller weapon and fired at Zephryn.

A cold breeze swept through the cave and then dissipated as Zephryn sank to the floor, unconscious.

* * * * *

Chloe did not have to feign her headache as they sped back to Righteous Angels territory. Kefton kept shooting her nervous glances. She would have liked to have put him at his ease, but nothing she could say would have helped. At this point her best option was keeping quiet.

Fortunately, Ulrik kept silent as well. She was doubly grateful for this. There was no telling what might have happened if she'd had to deal with him. She'd been staring out the window of the hover car and suddenly straightened up in her seat.

"This isn't the way to my house," she said.

"Gannon's not done with you yet," Ulrik taunted.

Chloe refused to rise to the bait. Clenching her teeth, she stayed silent.

When they reached the mine office Ulrik reached as though he was about to take her by the arm. Chloe leveled a stare at him and the ground beneath his feet trembled ever so slightly. She had the satisfaction of seeing a flash of fear in his eyes before something ugly replaced it.

Gannon was sitting at a bank of monitors when they reached his office. "Well done, Chloe," he said, turning to greet them. "An excellent job."

"I did what you wanted, stolen the livelihood from all those innocent people. Now let my mother go."

"Oh, I think not. As I said before, this was just a test. Your true task will be waiting for you tomorrow. And I've even found some added incentive for you to co-operate." He motioned to one of the monitors.

Chloe stepped closer. It was without surprise she saw Zephryn, pacing back and forth in a cell like room.

Chapter Twenty-seven

Zephryn stopped pacing and turned to face the door as he heard the lock disengage. A man dressed in a grey, non-descript uniform filled the doorway.

"Get back," he ordered, motioning with his weapon even though Zephryn was already well back from the door. "You're getting some company."

With a shrug, he raised his hands in mock surrender and backed up until his legs hit the cot against the wall behind him. When the man was satisfied he was far enough away from the door, he opened it wider and then thrust someone through, slamming the door shut again. Zephryn caught Chloe as she stumbled against him, turning the catch into a hug.

"Are you all right?" he asked.

She hugged him back. "I'm so sorry," she said, face buried in his chest.

"For what?"

"For this." She raised her head to look at him. "For you becoming embroiled in my troubles."

"It's not your fault." He kissed her gently. "We both know

who's to blame for this." He drew her down to sit with him on the bed. "I'm sorry I wasn't there for you."

She sighed. "You couldn't have helped. In fact, it might have made things worse. If Gannon—" she broke off what she was going to say.

"What's the matter?"

"I don't want to say the wrong thing in case he's listening. I know he has a camera in here - he can watch what goes on from his office."

"I suspected as much," he told her.

"Is that why you're still here?" She framed the question in such a way that he could answer without giving anything away.

"There's some kind of a current running through the walls of this place," he told her. "It acts as a security field. Gannon may be able to see into this cell, but I doubt very much if he can hear. Still, it doesn't hurt to be careful."

Chloe tried extending her awareness beyond the cell and found herself blocked. She shivered and tried not to panic. "I'm cut off from the earth!"

"It'll be all right." Zephryn put a comforting arm around her. "We'll get through this . . . somehow. I've survived worse."

"I think this is going to get much worse before it gets better." A tear made its way unnoticed down her cheek. "He had me shut down the Lightning Strike mine, and now he's trying to decide what he wants me to do next."

He frowned."What do you mean, shut it down?"

"I created fissures in the rock beneath the mine and caused the tunnels to collapse. The entire mine is just a pile of rubble now. It won't be cost effective to dig it out - it's totally gone."

She sagged against him so she could whisper in his ear, and told him what she did to make sure there was minimal loss of life.

He tightened his hold on her just enough to show his approval, and then asked, "What do you think he has planned next for you?"

"I'm almost afraid to wonder," she said. And then, in case Gannon was listening, she added, "Collapsing the Lightning Strike took so much out of me . . . I don't think I'd be able to do the same thing to one of the larger mines."

"Maybe trying wouldn't be a bad thing," he told her.

She pulled away enough to look askance at him. "How would that be a good thing?"

"If you burn yourself out trying to shut down one of the bigger mines then Gannon won't be able to use you again."

"Do you think that's even possible?" she asked in alarm.

"I don't see why not," he said with a slight shake of his head.

She realized he was speaking for Gannon's benefit and relaxed a bit. "It might be a good thing at that," she said, playing along. "Although I would hate to lose my abilities over such pettiness."

"Did Gannon at least let you speak with your mother?"

"He showed her to me, although I could not speak with her." Despite her best efforts to hold them back, her eyes filled with tears. "She's in the cell next to ours . . . he has her in some kind of glass coffin with wires going into it."

Zephryn put both arms around her and held her. "It sounds like a life pod," he told her. "That's a good thing. It means she'll be safe until you've done whatever it is he wants you to do."

"She looked like she was already dead."

"No," he reassured her. "Not dead. Her bodily functions have been suspended until she's released from the pod. If it's a medical pod it might even be helping her."

Chloe didn't respond, but her tears stopped.

Zephryn eased her down onto the cot. "You've had a long day, "he told her. "You need to rest."

"I don't know if I can. I don't think I'll rest again until this nightmare is over."

He lay down beside her. By moving onto their sides and spooning together, they could both just fit on the cot.

"You're exhausted. You're body knows it, even if your head doesn't."

"Maybe just a short rest," she murmured, eyes closed.

Zephryn held her close, smiling faintly at how quickly her breathing evened out as she fell asleep. While he hadn't exactly lied to her about being in a situation worse than this, he doubted he could compare what they were going through now with his escape from the compound.

For one thing, he wasn't the only one who escaped the compound, and it wasn't exactly an escape. He'd been part of the group Dr. Arjun had chosen to save, so he wasn't alone as they moved through the erupting volcano. And by the time they'd reached the other side, help had been waiting.

In this situation they were alone. The energy field that prevented him from using his wind outside of the room also prevented him from contacting Da'nat. Was the Ilezie even aware of what was going on? Martin had his own problems dealing with Gannon, and Granny was pretty much a wild card.

But they had two things going for them. Gannon didn't

know just how powerful Chloe really was, and had no idea Zephryn was an Elemental too. There had to be some way of working this to their advantage.

* * * * *

"Gra'anna!" Da'nat shouted with both his mind and his voice. "Show yourself."

Something wasn't right - not with her, not with Zephryn. He could feel it. Gra'anna was an ancient, he was just a youngling by comparison, and he owed her a certain measure of respect. But she was manipulating them all to her own end, whatever that was.

Even when they were apart he could still sense Zephryn, feel his emotions. His presence was like an itch in the back of his mind. But now that itch was gone and though he would have felt it had Zephryn died, it was disconcerting, to say the least, to not even have a sense of where he was.

When the survivors of Dr. Arjun's experiments arrived on Ardraci, the call went out for Ilezie mentors. Da'nat had just reached his tenth syllable, the age of adulthood for an Ilezie. So in that respect, he and Zephryn were of an age. Under normal circumstances he would have had to wait years before given charge of an Ardraci, but the situation with the sudden influx of Elementals worked in his favour.

Zephryn would probably be surprised to learn that Da'nat was with him by choice, not because he was obliged to be. Da'nat had liked the young man's spirit, his adventurous nature. Though he was expected to keep his distance, he found it difficult at times, enjoying the challenge of guiding Zephryn. Or at least trying to.

"Gra'anna! I know you can hear me."

There was a wuff of displaced air behind him and he turned to find her standing there. Though she was still in the form of an old woman, she radiated a sense of her true age, almost like an aura.

"Your young friend is safe, more or less," she said.

"Why can't I feel him?"

"Gannon has him hidden behind an electrical current. Even I'm having a hard time sensing him."

"And just how did Gannon get a hold of him?"

She sighed. "It happened purely by accident. I had one of Chloe's friends hide him away and it was just bad luck the place he chose was one Gannon had under surveillance."

"This is what comes from meddling," Da'nat said bitterly. "The Ilezie—"

"The Ilezie." She snorted. Moving over to the lounge area, she took a seat. "Did you know that in the beginning the Ardraci believed us to be gods? And further, for a time we allowed it."

Confused, Da'nat opened his mouth and quickly shut it again.

"That's right." She nodded. "When we first chose the Ardraci to receive the elemental gifts they thought we were gods come to bless them."

"What changed?" he asked, curious despite himself. What she spoke of came from a time that pre-dated the collective memories of their people. While the Ardraci held the Ilezie in high regard, they certainly no longer thought of them as gods.

She shrugged. "The elementals were created as part of the Trine Prophecy - how could they be the salvation of us all if they thought of themselves as lesser beings?"

"Trine Prophecy?"

"The Great Trine! Handed down to us by the Ashardaean Silversouls, the same ones who prophesized the coming of the Kohl-trin. What ails the Ilezian Keeper that you could be sent out so lacking in knowledge?"

Da'nat felt a stirring of umbrage. Who was she to chastise him? She was no longer even a true Ilezie. "We have not had a Keeper for centuries," he said stiffly.

"Ah!" she said, as though that was the answer to everything. "It is no wonder things are such a mess," she muttered.

Temper beginning to fray, Da'nat opened his mouth to make a quick retort but she shook her head, waving an all-too human hand at him. His anger ran from him like water and he felt the first stirring of fear. How had she done that?

"Forgive me," she said. "The Trine Prophecy is the reason we're here. The First Trine predicted the end of Ilezaire and the destruction of all, the Second saw to the creation of the Elementals, and the Third sent us from our home to await the Five Who Are One."

"We knew only to search for the one," Da'nat told her.

"Five of us set out, each to await one of the Five. Each of us ready to make the ultimate sacrifice when the time comes."

"I don't understand," Da'nat whispered.

She looked at him, but he did not think it was him she was seeing. "We were connected, just as the Five Who Are One are connected. When I first sensed the energy pulse drawing near I knew our time had come. I tried to reach out to the others, but there was only shadows."

A shiver went down Da'nat's spine. "What does that mean?"

"I do not know. But I look to the future and see only fear and darkness."

* * * * *

After several hours of a fitful sleep, Zephryn and Chloe were awake and sitting side by side on the bed when there was a noise outside the door. There was a distinct sound of the lock being disengaged before the door opened and an armed guard gestured to Chloe.

"Gannon wants to talk with you."

Zephryn gave her hand a reassuring squeeze and she stood.

"I want to see my mother first," she declared.

"Sorry," said the guard, looking genuinely sympathetic. "I have my orders."

"He doesn't dare let anything happen to your mother," Zephryn said quietly. "I'm not enough leverage to ensure your co-operation."

She opened her mouth to disagree and then thought better of it. "You're right," she agreed instead. "Zephryn, I . . ."

"I'll be fine," he said.

Chloe nodded and followed the guard out of the cell.

Zephryn tried to listen to their footsteps as they walked away but the walls of the cell were too thick. Or maybe it was the energy field that made it sound proof. With a sigh he drew his legs up onto the bed and adopted the meditative pose Da'nat had taught him. He needed to come up with a plan.

When they brought him here, he had hoped he'd be allowed to talk to Chloe, if for no other reason than to make sure she was all right. He figured the only reason she'd been put in this cell with him was so Gannon could see for himself how attached she was too him. It was all about leverage.

That Tierra was being kept in the room next to his was a stroke of luck. He was sorry it upset Chloe so much to see her mother in a life pod, but that was actually a bonus. The life support units were stand alone, and anti-grav was built into them. Gannon had done them a huge favour; moving her was going to be easy.

Getting out of this room would be easy too, thanks to his friend Kiravani. Picking locks was something of a hobby for his friend, knowledge he was more than willing to share. The lock on this door was nothing, compared to the security locks on the doors in the compound.

But he needed to have patience. He'd have to time his escape just right, hoping that Gannon would be distracted by whatever it was he was having Chloe do this time. Once he was through the door he should be able to contact Da'nat for help, maybe have him get a hold of Granny to enlist the aid of Chloe's friends.

Timing was going to be crucial.

He worried about Chloe being closeted with Gannon again. Could Gannon have figured out what he wanted her to do next? If he had, then it was unlikely he'd see her until she'd completed her task. And if the attack on the Lightning Strike mine was just a test, as Gannon implied, there was no telling what he'd have her do as the actual price of her mother's freedom. And was there going to be a price for his freedom as well?

Not that he for a moment believed it would be that easy with Gannon. No, he was not the type to let a useful tool like Chloe slip through his fingers, no matter what it took to keep her. And even if his word could be trusted, he'd find some other way to keep her in line - proper medical aid for her mother, threats against her friends . . .

Chapter Twenty-eight

Zephryn paced within the confines of the cell, ignoring the tray of food one of the guards brought. There was an awful lot of food on it. It gave him the hope that maybe it was meant for two.

His hope was realized when a short time later the lock on the door disengaged and it opened. One of the guards entered and held his weapon trained on him.

"Over there," the guard motioned with his weapon.

Zephryn dutifully moved to the side of the room furthest from the door.

The weapon was raised a fraction higher as he made an involuntary movement when a second guard carried in Chloe's limp form. She was set carefully on the cot and he backed away again. Zephryn hurried over to sit beside her.

"What did you do to her?" He looked up at the guard angrily.

"Wasn't me," the man said gruffly. "Gannon used some kind of drug on her. She's fine, she just needs to sleep it off." And with that he left, slamming the door and locking it behind him.

Zephryn's jaw clenched. Had it not been for the current infusing the cell . . . The guards were just fortunate that even with the cell door open his wind was blocked. Although to be fair they were only following orders, and at that the one carrying Chloe hadn't looked happy about it.

He glanced down at Chloe, brushing a strand of hair off her face. She stirred, but didn't awaken. For the next hour — perhaps it was longer, he had no way of knowing — he sat beside her, watching her sleep. Keeping alert for any signs of distress.

When she showed signs of waking up he glanced at the tray the guard had brought in earlier. Snagging the bottle that had been included, he uncorked it and took a sniff, then a cautious taste. As far as he could tell it held nothing more sinister than water.

Chloe's eyes fluttered, then opened. "Zephryn?" she whispered.

"Here." He helped her to sit up and held the bottle to her mouth. "Drink this. You need to re-hydrate."

She obediently took a drink and then took a good look around. It was pretty obvious when she became fully awake. She paled, fighting back the tears that sprang to her eyes, then her mouth tightened in anger. He got out of the way as she swung her legs over the side of the cot to sit up properly.

"He drugged me!" she spat out, thoroughly incensed. "That bastard drugged me with some kind of truth drug. That weasel Ulrik's suggestion, of course."

"Do you remember what he asked you?" Zephryn asked, a cold feeling in the pit of his stomach. He'd heard of drugs like that, and often those on whom they'd been used held little, or no, memory of what they'd said afterwards.

"Yes," she said bitterly. "I remember everything he asked me." She looked over at him. "He knows everything I can do, and just how powerful I am."

"Even we don't know that for certain," he told her quietly.

"He asked about you, too," she said, shoulders sagging. "He knows you're the pilot of the ship that broke through the security net, and that the ship is hidden away."

"It's all right," he said, pulling her into a comforting embrace.

"He doesn't know you're an elemental too," she whispered as she rested her head on his shoulder.

"He was bound to find out about your abilities sooner or later," he said aloud, for the benefit of anyone who might be listening.

"It would have been better if it had been later," she said with a sigh. "After he released my mother."

His arm tightened fractionally in acknowledgement. They sat that way for a few more moments, then he loosened his hold on her. She looked up at him, a question in her eyes.

"You need to eat," he told her.

"No," she shook her head. "I'm not—"

"You have to eat, to keep your strength up," he told her firmly. "And I'm not talking about your elemental strength. Your body needs fuel."

She sighed heavily as he reached for the tray, setting it down between them. Under his watchful gaze she nibbled half-heartedly at a roll. He waited until she broke it open and laid a piece of meat and cheese in between the halves before helping himself.

"Has he given you any hint of what he's going to expect you to do for him next?"

"Not really, no. Although he did seem quite interested in my ability to draw ore out of the earth."

Zephryn frowned. According to what Da'nat had told him, this was one of the most dangerous aspects of her gift. Extracting too much of the wrong thing could trigger a natural cascade effect that would be too unpredictable to put a stop to.

"You should try and rest some more," he suggested.

"I don't think I can," she told him. "I'm too worried about what Gannon's going to make me do."

"I am too," he admitted.

"I just wish I could get this over with."

* * * * *

The waiting seemed interminable. At first they sat side by side on the cot, Chloe leaning on Zephryn for support. Eventually, unable to stay still any longer, he got up to pace. She pulled her legs up to sit crossed legged as she watched him.

"Are you all right?" she asked at last.

He paused in the act of turning and glanced at her, giving her a wan smile. "I'm fine. This room isn't much smaller than the one I had in the compound." He came back over to sit beside her again. "It's strange, being confined never bother me until I learned what freedom was."

"Tell me about it," she said. "I need something to take my mind off things. What was it like growing up in this compound of yours?"

He scooted back so he could lean his back against the wall. Chuckling, he said, "I don't know where to start."

"Well, start with your parents. What were they like?"

"I don't know; I never knew them. None of us knew our parents."

"Did you never get to see them?" Chloe put a hand on his arm, unable to hide her shock.

"It was the way things were." He shrugged as though it was of no great matter. "I think I told you we were part of a breeding program?"

"Yes, but still . . ."

"Like I told you before, babies remained with their mothers for the first two years - and I think that was only allowed to save on nursing staff. At two we were removed to the nurseries where we were watched over by the medical staff. At five, we were moved to dormitories, one for the girls and one for the boys."

"It sounds so cold."

"You have no idea." He went on to explain in detail how their days were filled with lessons and how they were kept in year groups. How they were given designations that were burned into their wrists instead of names. Boys and girls had lessons together until puberty, when they were separated.

"What about friends?" Chloe asked.

"Friends were discouraged," he told her, then smiled. "Although that didn't stop Kiravini and I from maintaining a friendship. But we were very careful about it."

"It shouldn't have to be that way!" she protested.

"No, it shouldn't. Around the time of *tespiro* we began having classes on breeding and what was expected of us . . ." His voice trailed off as he remembered.

Chloe took one look at his face and closed her mouth on the question she was about to ask.

He looked at her sadly. "You may find this hard to believe, but although I've had a great deal of experience having sex, I've had very little when it comes to making love."

At that she cracked a smile. "I've no complaints so far."

He laughed, as she hoped he would, and put his arm around her for a hug.

"For those who survived their *tespiro*, that was the total sum of their lives - one cold and impersonal breeding after another. Offspring taken from their mothers to start the cycle all over again. Even our gifts were suppressed - we had no idea what we were."

"That's horrible!" The words escaped before Chloe could stop them.

"It didn't seem like it at the time. We knew no other life; to us it was normal."

"That doesn't make it right."

"No, it doesn't," he said with a sigh, leaning his head back to rest against the wall.

Chloe was quiet for a few moments, trying to wrap her mind around what Zephryn had been through. If her mother hadn't escaped from the ship, would that have been her life as well?

"How did you escape?" she asked. "You said something about a journey through a mountain and a volcano erupting . . ."

"The man who ran the breeding program, Dr. Uri Arjun, was a madman. Both the Ardraci and the Illezi had been after him for years. They finally stumbled across his location, but he'd built his compound into the base of a volcano - it was far too dangerous to make a frontal assault, too many innocent lives could be lost."

"Go on," she said when he paused. "How did they get your people out?"

"Arjun was not only mad, he was paranoid as well. He'd already started a plan to move the compound to what he considered a more secure location. And he thought he was close to his goal, so he was only taking those he deemed necessary with him."

"What was his goal? Wait—" She sat up straight and looked at him. "You said only those he deemed necessary. What about the others?"

"By this time he knew he'd been discovered and his plan was to disappear into the cave system riddling the volcano. The volcano was in danger of erupting and he'd intended for the lava to take care of those he left behind and those coming after him."

"He wasn't a man, he was a monster!"

"Now on that, we're in complete agreement." He pulled her back so they were sitting side by side, leaning against the wall, his arm around her.

"One hundred and thirteen people perished in the volcano," he said softly. "Five more were unable to adapt to freedom and ended their lives before they could be stopped."

"Oh, Zephryn," she said, voice laden with emotion she couldn't express. "I can't even begin to tell you how sorry I am for what you've been through."

His arm tightened around her. "I can't honestly say that I am."

"What?" Her head lifted and she looked at him, appalled.

"It's led me to you," he said.

"Oh! I—oh." She blushed faintly. "I don't know what to say."

He grinned and closed his eyes.

Again they sat together quietly for a few moments, but Chloe had too many questions to remain silent for long.

"Can I ask you something?"

"You can ask me anything," he said, without opening his eyes.

"This breeding program . . . that is . . ." She took a deep breath and finished in a rush. "Does that mean you have children?"

"Probably. That was the whole purpose behind it." He opened his eyes and turned his head to look at her. "The records that were saved were incomplete. I left Ardraci before finding out for certain." Here he hesitated. "It's not that I don't care, you understand. But given the way I was raised, what do I have to offer a child?"

"I think you would make an amazing father," she told him, leaning her head back and closing her eyes.

He stared at her a moment in surprise, then a grin slid across his face as he, too, leaned his head back again.

Chapter Twenty-nine

Chloe was ready to scream by the time Gannon finally sent for her. Although being confined did not unduly bother her, being cut off from the earth was making her extremely uncomfortable.

She and Zephryn talked, they dozed, they took turns pacing and sat in companionable silence. Having him with her made her confinement barely tolerable. She wanted to be outside with the sun on her face and Zephryns's wind in her hair. She wanted to feel the earth beneath her feet, to sink her awareness deep within it to make green things grow. Most of all, she wanted to make love to Zephryn, but she was all too aware of the camera's unblinking stare.

When the lock on the door disengaged, they were sitting side by side on the cot again, resting their backs against the wall.

"Gannon wants to see you," the guard said.

"Of course," she said, getting to her feet. Glancing back at Zephryn she said, "I'll see what I can do to get you out of here."

"Be careful," he said.

She didn't want to leave him like this. Too late she wished they'd spent more time trying to come up with some kind of a plan.

"Watch your control," he added. "Especially before attempting any large projects."

Somewhat mystified at his warning, Chloe nodded anyway. Why would he tell her to watch her control, unless … maybe he was suggesting she pretend her control wasn't very good. It would be easy enough to make mistakes and blame it on lack of control.

No, wait! He'd specifically mentioned watching it before attempting any large projects. He was asking her to let him know when she was about to start whatever task Gannon had in store for her. Hopefully he had a plan for escape, one that included her mother.

One last, lingering look and she was through the door, one guard locking it behind her while the other one led the way down the corridor. She paused outside her mother's room.

"You can tell Gannon I'm not going anywhere until I see for myself that my mother is still all right," she informed her escort.

The younger of the pair looked like he was about to argue, but the older one was already using his communicator to contact Gannon.

"She says she wants to check on her mother," he was saying. He listened for a moment and looked over at Chloe. "Gannon says she'll be fine as long as you co-operate."

"You tell Gannon I need to check on her for myself. If I'm worried about how she's doing I may make mistakes, and he wouldn't want that now, would he?"

He replayed her message and then closed his communicator. "All right. You can go in. But only for a moment."

He nodded at the younger guard who opened the door for her.

It was unlocked - there was no danger of Tierra trying to leave.

Despite her insistence this was what she wanted, Chloe hesitated before moving slowly towards the life pod. It still looked too much like a glass coffin for comfort, but Zephryn assured her it would keep her mother alive, and she trusted him.

Her mother looked so fragile lying inside the case. She rested a hand on it - it was cold and hard to the touch. It would have been comforting to hear a shushing sound of oxygen being cycled through it, or the whir of machinery at work, but it was silent. As hard as she stared, she could detect no faint rise and fall of Tierra's chest. It was like she was frozen.

"Time's up," the guard said gruffly.

He seemed a little shaken at the sight of her mother in the life pod but Chloe knew better than to think she could count on his help. Gannon owned these people. Without a word she turned away, suppressing a shiver as the door clanged shut behind her.

When they reached Gannon's office, the guard knocked on the door, waiting for the order to enter. The door was opened for Chloe, but the guards stayed outside.

Gannon's desk was littered with geological surveys, as was the round table in the corner. Gannon himself seemed to be in a suspiciously good mood. In fact, he was looking very pleased with himself.

"My dear Chloe," he greeted her. "I hope you found everything with your mother to your satisfaction?"

"It's hard to tell, what with her being in that machine."

"You'll just have to take my word for it," he said. "Or perhaps your spaceman friend is familiar with life pods and can explain their workings to you."

"You need to let him go. He has nothing to do with any of this."

"Oh, indeed, my girl. That's just his bad luck now, isn't it?" He gestured towards a chair at the round table, taking the one opposite for himself. "Have a seat."

"Where's your new best friend?" she asked, noting Ulrik's absence.

"Never fear, he'll be along shortly," Gannon said. "He's procuring some special equipment for me."

"Why don't we cut to the chase," she suggested. "What do you want from me?"

He leaned forward, shaking his head slightly. "Chloe, Chloe, Chloe. There's no need for such hostility. With my knowledge and your abilities, we could have an extremely profitable partnership."

"It's never going to happen Gannon. Just tell me what it's going to take to release my mother and Zephryn."

He sat back with a sigh. "I didn't think you'd agree, but I had to try." He gestured to the report sitting on top of the pile of papers. "Are you familiar with the ore that's known as pantarium?"

She frowned. "Every miner is. It's the rarest mineral known - key in the production of fuel for transwarp ships."

"What would you say if I told you we were sitting on top of one of the largest deposits of pantarium I've ever heard of?"

Chloe started to get a sick feeling in the pit of her stomach. Pantarium was not only rare, its volatile nature made it the most dangerous substance to mine. Because of this it was never extracted from populated worlds. "I'd say there was probably a very good reason why no one's tried to mine it before."

"That's because no one's ever had what I have," he said, dismissing her concerns. "They never had you."

Chloe stared at Gannon as though seeing him for the first time. Clearly he was letting his greed overcome his good sense. He couldn't possibly be about to suggest what she thought he was . . . could he? The sick feeling in her stomach grew as he slid a geological survey in front of her.

"This shows everything you'll need to know for the extraction of the ore."

She looked at him, shock written plainly on her face. "You expect me to extract pantarium? Just like that." She snapped her fingers.

"Why not? I heard from your own lips that extracting ore is one of your powers. This will be no different than any of the other precious ores we mine."

"You're insane! You must know that there's a reason robots are used to mine pantarium. The slightest miscalculation . . ." She shuddered. The slightest miscalculation could blow them all to hell at best, blow the entire world apart at worst.

"Which is why you need to be very careful," he said with a smirk.

Chloe opened her mouth to continue arguing, then snapped it shut again. There was no point - it was like talking to a wall.

Picking up the survey map, she studied it carefully. It was a huge deposit. She wouldn't be surprised if it had been earmarked by the mining companies for when this planet was mined out. Once everyone was gone one of the companies was probably planning on coming back for it.

Even a small portion would make Gannon a king. He'd marked an area close to the Righteous Angels where the pantarium could be drawn up. Still, it was an incredibly risky procedure.

Frowning, she traced the vein as it narrowed to a mere thread, winding its way downwards, many leagues beneath them until it ran off the page.

"Where's the next page?" she asked.

Wordlessly, he flipped through the pile and pulled out a second page. Chloe's eyes narrowed as she looked at it, then she paled.

"Do you see how far down this vein goes?"

"It's not a continuous vein," he protested. "There are . . . gaps."

"Not large enough to prevent a chain reaction should something go wrong!" The vein of pantarium snaked its way downwards until it petered out with only a thin crust of rock between it and the core of the planet.

"Then you'd better hope that nothing goes wrong," he snapped.

Chloe shivered at the maniacal look in his eye. There was no chance of him being swayed, no matter how dangerous this task could be.

"I want you to promise that if I do this for you, then no more games. I will extract enough pantarium to keep you in riches for the rest of your life, but you will let Zephryn take my mother to his ship and then you will allow us to leave this world."

"Extract enough pantarium to make it worth my while and you are free to do whatever you wish."

Chloe wished with all her heart she could believe him.

* * * * *

Da'nat watched Gra'anna as she shifted in her seat.

"It was no accident I was chosen for this mission, and by extension Zehpryn, is it?"

She hesitated before answering and he had the feeling she was choosing her words carefully.

"If you were chosen," she said finally, "It was by the Great Consciousness itself. My knowledge of such things is somewhat … uncertain."

"What does that mean?"

"It means I am old," she snapped. "And I am not as I once was. All I know for certain is that should we survive the next few hours, then Chloe is the chosen Earth Elemental and Zephryn is her anchor."

"Anchor?" Da'nat all but pounced on the word.

"Each of the Five will have an anchor to bind them to the here and now."

That wasn't answering his question, but he let it go for now. "Have you seen how this all will end?"

She gave a bitter laugh. "Despite my part in how this began, the future has become dark and I do not know whether it is because there is no future, or I just cannot see it."

Gra'anna sat up suddenly. "I can feel her . . . I can feel her fear. Soon it will begin."

"What can we do to help?"

"I have already meddled over-much," she admitted. "In trying to hurry things along, I may have made matters worse."

"I am not sure how things could be worse," he told her.

"You've been patient for centuries, how can you be lacking in patience this close to the end?"

"You're a sharp one, you are," she gave a laugh, then her smile faded. "It is a terrible thing, to have been able to see the future all your life and then suddenly the visions stop. For centuries I have seen future possibilities spread out before me, the choices, the potentials, stretching out like a great web ... It is disconcerting to see only darkness now."

"The body you're in, it's failing, isn't it?" he asked suddenly. It would explain much about what was wrong with her.

"Yes." No hesitation, no evasions, just one simple answer.

"Will you be able to return with us?"

"I . . . do not know. But I would like to see this through, if I can."

"I dislike waiting," he told her.

At that she cracked a smile. "As do I, youngling. As do I."

Chapter Thirty

Zephryn alternated pacing with meditating. Every time he made the switch he'd surreptitiously glance up at the camera tucked up in the corner of the ceiling near the air vent. The lack of privacy did not unduly bother him, although even when he'd lived in the compound he hadn't been monitored this closely.

He might not have noticed the camera at all if it hadn't been for the tell-tale amber light that glowed when it was in use. Chloe had only confirmed his suspicions of what it was.

When Chloe was in the cell with him the amber light was a constant. But when he was alone it appeared to come and go at regular intervals. He could only surmise that watching him when he was alone wasn't nearly as interesting as watching him interact with Chloe.

His gut told him that this was it. He wouldn't be seeing her again until she'd completed whatever task it was that Gannon had set for her this time. Now all he could do is wait for her signal - provided she'd understood what he meant when he told her to watch her control. If she could cause an earth tremor, like the ones she inadvertently caused before, it would provide him with a window of opportunity.

It had been a spur of the moment suggestion. Why had he not thought of it earlier, when he could have explained to her that he intended on rescuing her mother? Now he could only hope that once he was free of this room he'd be able to speak mind to mind with Da'nat and get a message to Chloe through him. Then she'd be free to take whatever action she deemed necessary to win free from Gannon.

He fingered the cuff on his wrist. While a few of the survivors from the compound opted to have the identification tattoos removed from their wrists, the majority kept them, a reminder of who they were. Some, like Zephryn, chose to keep the tattoo but concealed it beneath a metal or leather cuff.

His friend Kiravini wore a cuff even when he was in the compound. His had contained a powerful inhibitor - he'd had no idea of his immense power. Now his cuff held his lock picking tools, a fine set of instruments he designed himself.

Zephryn's cuff was identical to Ravi's, a gift from his friend. Though he would never be the master of locks Ravi was, he was confident the lock on the door to this cell would give him no trouble.

Now all he had to do was wait for the right moment to act.

* * * * *

The geological survey could only show so much. Chloe all but stared holes into the paper it was printed on. Unfortunately, it didn't give her the information she really needed - that would only be available once she was at the site itself.

She didn't have long to wait. As soon as Ulrik returned from whatever arrangements he'd been making, she was led to a specially outfitted cargo ship and flown to the extraction site. At least Gannon had taken precautions for the transportation of the pantarium - specially lined containers, easy enough for him to put together with supplies from the mine, were being unloaded by Ulrik.

Gannon had been disappointed to learn she couldn't just teleport the ore into their containers. She had no reason to lie to him. Bringing the ore to the surface would be a difficult enough task, once it was on the surface she would have limited ability to move it from place to place.

Though he did not have access to the special robots used for mining pantarium, he did have several that were capable of moving the ore into the containers. Chloe watched silently as he and Ulrik argued over the placement of the containers around the extraction site. Ulrik also argued about being used for manual labour when there were robots available. Obviously there was friction between the pair. Maybe it would be possible to use that to her advantage at some point.

The site was a gentle bowl surrounded by trees and rock, the ship parked to one side. The containers were laid on their sides in a semi-circle. Chloe was to bring the ore up to the surface and as close to the containers as possible. The robots could take over from there.

As Ulrik and Gannon argued over the placement of the containers, Chloe paced past the ship and back again. When she was within speaking distance of Gannon she stopped. "Have one of the containers placed over there," she told him, pointing to an area off to the side.

"Why there?"

"Because I've never done anything like this before and I'd like to try it without having to worry about blowing us all up first," she snapped.

He looked like he was going to argue with her but must have understood something of her body language because he gave the order. Ulrik glared at them, but did what he was told.

Sending her awareness into the earth, she searched for and identified several different minerals of equal mass to the pantarium. Under other circumstances she would have enjoyed trying to use her gift deliberately, but right now she was too conscious of how much was at stake. Gently she teased the minerals upwards, pulling at the ones she wanted, pushing others to take their place to avoid leaving air pockets.

The minerals she'd found were not as deep as the pantarium, but they gave her some idea of how far she was going to have to delve. This was a job that would be best done over the course of several days, but she knew Gannon would never agree to that.

It was slow work. Difficult but not impossible. The ground was not as stable as she would have liked, but she had no choice in the matter. At least it made it easier to send a tremor towards the building where Zephryn and her mother were being kept prisoner.

* * * * *

"It's time," Gra'anna said.

Da'nat looked at her blankly. "Time for what?"

"Time to unbury the ship."

He'd been afraid of this ever since he realized she had lost the ability to transfer to a new body. She had been human for so long it had affected her mind.

"We are buried under tonnes of earth," he told her gently. "We will have to hope that Chloe can unbury us again. I'm not even sure Zephryn's wind can remove all—"

"Do not patronize me! I haven't lost my mind." She pushed up from her seat and came to stand before him. "I don't know what they're teaching you younglings these days, but all you need to do is lend me your power. I'll do the rest."

"I don't . . ." his voice trailed off as he looked at her.

Power filled her eyes, sparking and snapping. Without a word he held his hands up, palms facing her. She held her palms to his and he almost flinched at the crackle of energy transferring from him to the ancient.

Gra'anna closed her eyes. The energy flickered along her skin, glowing lines snaking over her like lightning. In that moment Da'nat had a glimpse of what true power was.

There was a rumbling, a vibration. The ship trembled but Da'nat held fast. The rumbling increased and there was a sense of motion. When it stopped, Gra'anna slumped forward. Da'nat caught her and eased her into a chair. When he glanced out the viewport he could see the sky.

* * * * *

Zephryn was sitting cross-legged on the bed, meditating, when he felt it, the telltale trembling of the ground beneath him. It was late in the day, as far as he could tell. All he knew for certain was that he was about to snap from the waiting. But was it really a signal from Chloe, or just coincidence? Did it really matter at this point?

Glancing up at the camera he saw that its light was off. Perfect timing. He unsnapped the leather cuff from around his wrist and slid his thumbnail along the hidden seam. So unobtrusive, so easy to miss. He was fortunate the guards had been content with their cursory search for weapons.

Even as harmless as it appeared, he'd have never been allowed to keep the cuff if Kiravini's wife Taja had been in charge. She took her job as head of Ardraci security very seriously. In her hands, anything could be made into a weapon, even something as innocuous as a set of lock-picking tools.

He went over to the door, squatting down to better study the lock. After a moment, he extracted a pair of slim tools and closed the pouch again so the others didn't fall out.

Carefully, he inserted one of them into the lock, then wriggled the other one in on an angle. There was a click, and he stopped what he was doing. For several moments he waited, but he heard nothing else. No sound at all from the other side of the door.

"It can't be that easy," he muttered. But apparently it was. He tried the door and it opened effortlessly under his touch.

Straightening, he poked his head cautiously though the opening. He saw a short corridor, doors set along it at intervals, but no guards.

The second he stepped through he could feel his wind again, and went almost weak with relief.

Da'nat?

It is almost time.

Zephryn was almost afraid to ask time for what. He couldn't help feel that it was much more than whatever Chloe and Gannon were up to. *Can you get a message to Chloe, let her know I'm safe and her mother soon will be?*

There was a pause, then, *I cannot.*

He let out a breath, not quite a curse but not quite a sigh. He'd hoped that armed with the knowledge her mother was safe, Chloe could stop whatever it was Gannon had her doing, maybe even get away herself.

You must bring the mother to the ship.

Zephryn was already opening the room beside his. As Chloe had said, Tierra was ensconced in a life pod of some kind, though he was unfamiliar with the design.

I'm not sure how to safely open this, he said, looking at the control panel.

Is it equipped with an anti-gravity device?

He checked along the bottom. *Yes, there's a standard anti-grav to move the pod.*

She will not be able to make the journey to the ship on her own, it would be best to transport her to the vessel while still in the life pod.

Zephryn looked askance at the coffin-sized life pod. *It's going to be difficult to be inconspicuous.*

It will not matter.

Not matter? He must not have heard that right. *Da'nat—*

Hurry.

Zephryn caught the sense of urgency from the voice in his head and took another look at the instrument panel of the pod. Fortunately there was an independent power source. Deftly he activated it and then disconnected the wiring that held the pod in place with no interruption of power. Activating the anti-gravs, he gave an experimental tug. The pod moved easily a few inches away from the wall - the whole unit was now independent.

Sending up a quick prayer of thanks to whatever deity might be listening, he pushed the life pod in front of him into the hallway. It was a little disconcerting, seeing Tierra's still form through the clear casing of the life pod. How was he going to explain what he was doing with her?

A few feet further and he stopped the anti-gravs to keep the pod in place while he searched through the rooms further along. Two of the rooms appeared to be empty offices, the third appeared to be a clerk's office, judging by the paperwork. He shook his head at the mess. Obviously, computer equipment to make his staff's lives easier was not high on Gannon's priority list.

The next door he tried opened into a store room. He helped himself to a jacket similar to what he'd seen the miners wear, a heavy tarp in a non-descript grey material, and a length of rope from a pile in a box on one of the shelves.

It didn't occur to him, until he was back at the life pod, that he should have looked for something to use as a weapon. Glancing back at the room, he shrugged. He'd just have to rely on his wind for defense - he wasn't very good with weapons anyway.

I don't suppose you could tell me which office is Gannon's? he asked Da'nat. The last thing he needed at this point was to run into the man.

He guards Chloe. He and another.

Probably that weasel Ulrik. After securing the tarp over the pod with the rope, he donned the jacket and continued on his way. He was still dressed in the casual clothing Granny had provided, and since Gannon wasn't around to stop him, decided to just brazen it out. Using the life pod to push open the outer door, he walked across the yard like he had every right to be there.

There were only a few people in the yard, and no one made a move to stop him. They seemed to be well trained to mind their own business - most barely even gave him a second glance. Still, he moved as quickly as he was able, considering the awkwardness of the life pod.

He breathed a little easier as he reached what passed for a road, and then tried to remember where he'd emerged from the woods when he'd journeyed from the ship back to Chloe's house. Was it through this opening here?

He stopped the life pod to check. Taking several steps off the road he realized this was not the way. It took three more stops before he thought he found a place that looked familiar. Praying for luck, he reactivated the anti-gravs and pushed the pod forward.

After a few minutes he topped a rise, glanced down and froze. This was definitely the right place, and there sat the ship, completely unburied.

He barely had enough time to recover from that shock, when the earth beneath his feet began to move.

Chapter Thirty-one

Chloe looked at the robot drones grouped together in the bowl created by the surrounding rock and soil and felt a chill. Even if she were successful in drawing the pantarium to the surface, she had her doubts about the drones being able to safely move it into the containers.

She tried one last time to make Gannon see reason. "There are many precious gems and metals at a depth that would make them too costly to try for. It would be so much better —"

"They would not fetch the price the pantarium would."

"No, but at least we'd be alive for you to enjoy the profit," she snapped.

"It's like she doesn't want to see her mother cured or her pilot, what was his name? Zephryn? released. I think she's stalling," Ulrik said.

"No one asked you," Gannon told him with a glare meant to quell. Ulrik glared right back.

"Even bringing up non-volatile ore so close to the mantle is dangerous. I've never done anything like this before and I could accidentally trigger a seismic reaction."

"Then you'd better be especially careful." Gannon was implacable in his greed.

In despair she looked at the five containers waiting to be filled. "You think over much of my abilities. What if I'm unable to extract enough ore for all of these?"

He shrugged. "Then you will keep at it until you can extract no more."

Even if the deposit was closer to the surface, this would be a dangerous operation. Fortunately the deposit was sizeable and the containers were not large. Such was the value of the ore that just one container would hold a small fortune of pantarium.

If it had been within her power she'd have warned the miners - not just at Righteous Angel, but the other mines as well - about what she was going to attempt so they could be prepared.

"I suggest you get on with it," Gannon said.

Chloe opened her mouth, then shut it again, leaving whatever she was about to say stillborn in her throat. There was just no reasoning with him. He would have what he would have, even if it meant the destruction of their world.

He was right about one thing though. At this point she was just stalling for time. She hoped the minor tremor she'd "accidentally" set off during her test run hadn't done too much damage. More, she hoped she hadn't weakened any of the natural faults in this area.

If something went wrong, would Zephryn be able to escape? And what about her mother? No, she had to put them from her mind. She couldn't allow herself to think of anything but the task at hand. Zephryn wouldn't just sit idly by - she had faith that he had some kind of plan to escape, and that he'd take her mother with him.

"I'm losing patience, Chloe."

She turned to him. "Let's get something straight here. Once I begin, under no circumstances are you to disturb me. You can't touch me or even talk to me. Any distraction that could compromise my concentration could be fatal for us all."

"Understood," he said, though she had the feeling he didn't fully believe her.

Mouth dry, Chloe moved to the center of the circle of containers. She wished she could have had one last moment with Zephryn, one last kiss. One last chance to tell him . . .

No, that was defeatist thinking. She had to stay positive. She could tell him how she felt when they saw each other again, once she succeeded in extracting the pantarium.

Kneeling down, she placed her hands palm down on the ground. Technically, she probably didn't need direct contact to accomplish her task, but the tactile sensation helped calm her.

She felt the sparse blades of grass, the prickly edges of the chokeweed that covered the ground here. Narrowing her focus she could feel the stones beneath the foliage, then the sharpness of the grit before it turned to earth.

Despite Gannon's obvious impatience, she took her time. Rushing things would only lead to making a mistake, which she could ill afford. Focus - she needed to focus. Don't think of anything but the task at hand.

As her awareness sank deeper and deeper into the earth she kept track of the natural fissures and channels. The less she had to manipulate the surrounding soil on the way back up, the better.

Her heart sank as she hit a hard-rock ledge. There was no going through it and she didn't dare try and move it, it could be catastrophic. The pantarium was somewhere below it and she could not quite tell how far.

She was already too deep, she could feel the reverberations of what she was doing radiating outwards along the naturally occurring fault lines. There was no way of knowing what kind of damage it was doing and she had not the energy to spare to try and dampen it.

Working her way around the ledge she continued downwards until she reached the closest deposit of pantarium. Slowly and carefully she coaxed the ore upwards along the path she'd created for it, leaving the veins of pantarium in the zaminyte and gansite it was threaded through. With any luck the additional rock would help keep it stable.

The ground shivered in front of the first container as the pantarium riddled ore pushed its way to the surface. Chloe sat back on her heels and swiped an arm across her face. Her forehead was beaded with sweat.

"It's not pure pantarium," Gannon said, clearly disappointed.

"That's what refineries are for," she snapped. "The containers you have are not capable of transporting pure pantarium."

His lips tightened but he knew she was right. "Proceed."

Chloe was able to raise enough ore to fill two containers before the vein she was working ran out. This is what she was afraid of, she was going to have to tap into the larger, and far less stable, deposit.

She hoped Zephryn had somehow managed to get himself and her mother safely to his ship.

* * * * *

After managing to fill a third container by feeding off the edges of the larger deposit, Chloe sat back on her heels. It was nerve wracking work - the slightest misjudgement could be catastrophic.

"What is it? What's wrong?" Gannon demanded.

"I need a break, that's what's wrong!" she told him. "Do you think this is easy?"

He eyed her dispassionately. "Ten minutes, then back to work. I want this finished before the sun sets."

Chloe nodded. "Do you have any water with you? I could use a drink."

He huffed out a breath, then dug out a bottle and tossed it to her.

"Thank you." She drank half of it down without stopping.

Idly she watched the drones sealing the three containers of pantarium riddled ore and move the containers into the hold of the ship Gannon had used to bring them here.

"This is going too slow," Ulrik whined. "I think—"

"You?" Gannon rounded on him. "You? Think? I warned you before that this is my operation and—"

"If it hadn't been for me you'd never have known what you had right under your nose!"

"You're right, but my gratitude only goes so far." Gannon pulled out a laser pistol.

Ulrik back peddled fast. "Wh—what are you doing?"

"You've just become expendable." There was a brilliant flash as Gannon shot him.

Chloe stared, open mouthed, as Ulrik's body slumped to the ground.

"All right. You've had enough time. Back to work."

Still she stared, frozen in shock.

Gannon shrugged, carelessly. "He outlived his usefulness. Perhaps you should see that you don't."

Shaken, Chloe resumed her kneeling position. Once again she rested her hands on the earth, sinking her awareness down, down towards the deposit of pantarium, pushing Gannon's callous way of dealing with his former partner from her mind.

It was easier this time, the earth below had a familiar feel to it. But again she took her time, checking one of the fault-lines that ran downwards at an angle. Was it larger than before? And those fractures . . . had they held that spiderweb of fissures? The ground began to tremble but there was no helping it. She would just have to compensate for it when she brought the ore back up.

Shrugging off a sense of foreboding, she focused on the task at hand. Her awareness touched the large pantarium deposit and her whole body jerked.

It was massive. And almost one hundred per cent pure. It was . . . it was almost a living thing. Chloe was filled with a sense of euphoria. It would be so easy to just lose herself in the sensation forever.

* * * * *

Zephryn secured Tierra in her life pod in the medical bay and then sought out Da'nat and Granny in the lounge. Somehow he hadn't been surprised to see her lurking near the hatch of the ship when he entered.

"I've secured the pod as best I could," he told them. "But I wasn't sure how to connect it to the ship's power so I left it on its own."

"That's fine," Da'nat told him. "It could very well be we won't need to connect it to the ship. I'll check on it later."

"We need to warn them," Granny said abruptly.

"Who?" Zephryn asked, confused.

"Everyone."

He glanced at Da'nat but the Ilezie seemed pre-occupied and didn't respond. "What about Martin?" he suggested.

Granny looked at him, a question in her eyes. There was something different about her, as though she'd undergone some kind of change.

"We can warn Martin - he'd know who to get in touch with at the other mines. I can—"

"No," she said suddenly. "I'll get in touch with Martin. You need to go to her."

That got a reaction from Da'nat. He seemed to come awake and looked at her sharply. "No! It is far too dangerous!"

"He is the only one who can do this."

"I will not allow you to put him in danger. You have said it yourself, you have meddled too much already."

They glared at each other. If Zephryn didn't know better, he'd have thought Da'nat was taking orders from her. What was going on?

"What are you two talking about?" His annoyance leaked into his tone.

"Chloe needs you," Granny told him.

"No! It is too dangerous!" Da'nat was adamant. "She is losing herself in the earth. He will not be able to reach her before she begins to take on the characteristics of the pantarium."

Zephryn heard nothing other than the fact that Chloe needed him.

"Where is she?"

"You're right, it will be dangerous," Granny said to Da'nat. "There is no time to waste. We must send him to her - together."

Zephryn looked from one to the other. What was she talking about? And why was Da'nat glaring at her as though she was revealing something she shouldn't?

"Just tell me where she is," he told them. He didn't have time for whatever game they were playing.

"You know it is the only way," Granny said softly.

Da'nat was clearly unhappy. "Then it must be now," he said. "And I would have your word that should he not be able to reach her, we will bring him back."

"Agreed." Turning to Zephryn, she said, "Stand here, between us."

Though he had a thousand questions, Zephryn did as he was told. He caught their sense of urgency. Questions could wait, Chloe couldn't. Of that he was absolutely sure.

They faced each other, Zephryn between them, and held their arms slightly away from their sides, palms facing outwards. He could feel some kind of energy building, a pressure that made his ears pop.

He blinked and suddenly he was somewhere outside, the ground beneath his feet trembling. Chloe was several feet away, kneeling on the ground. And she was beginning to glow.

Chapter Thirty-two

When Tierra had first realized that one of her daughter's gifts was the extraction of ore, she had warned her of the many dangers of such a process, one of them being the seductive nature of certain minerals. And there was no mineral more seductive than pantarium.

Even had Chloe remembered her mother's cautions, she might not have been able to resist the pull of the pantarium. She was tired, both mentally and physically, no match for its insidious promises.

She could feel it where it pooled in its rocky cradle. The pantarium was speaking to her. Chloe was sure that if she just listened closely she could understand what it was saying. It was silky smooth; it was fiery hot. What had been a whisper from the pantarium laced ore was a scream from the pure pantarium.

It promised her peace beyond measure. She had only to merge her consciousness with it. Give up any idea of 'self'. And there's where the true danger lay, the danger that came from submerging the consciousness too far.

She was ready to be one with it, but something was holding her back, anchoring her to the mundane.

* * * * *

Zephryn fought to keep his balance as the earth beneath his feet gave another massive shudder. Gannon was off to his left, watching Chloe with a laser pistol held loosely in his hand. Near to the transport ship was Ulrik's cooling body. It looked like he was no longer Gannon's new best friend.

"Chloe," he called, taking a step towards her. "Whatever you're doing, you need to stop."

There was no response, although the air around her seemed to pulse. He knew better than to try and touch her, but he took another step closer. That drew Gannon's attention and the laser pistol was turned in his direction.

"How did you get here?" he demanded.

"You need to leave this place, now," Zephryn told him.

"Who are you to give me orders?" Gannon blustered. He waved the laser pistol at Zephryn for emphasis. "I'm in charge here and—"

Zephryn used his wind to pluck the weapon from his hand and whirl it away.

"Go. Now," he said, punctuating each word with a nudge from his wind. "While you still can."

Gannon's face was ashen but he stood his ground. "I'm not going anywhere until I get what I came for."

Zephryn turned back to Chloe, who was radiating a silver glow. She'd never looked so beautiful, but it was a cold, terrifying beauty.

"Chloe, you need to stop what you're doing."

At the sound of his voice she turned in his direction, her focus split between him and what she was doing. "Zephryn? My mother?"

"She's fine. Or she will be. She's on the ship, waiting for us."

"You need to go. Leave me here."

He took a step closer. "You know that's not going to happen."

She opened her mouth to reply, then her eyes widened as she spotted something behind him. He turned to see Gannon starting towards him with a wicked looking knife. But the other man only made it a few steps before the ground opened up underneath him and then closed up again, the earth muffling Gannon's screams.

Zephryn turned back to Chloe, too shocked for words.

She stared back at him, a stricken expression in her eyes. "By the earth," she whispered. "What have I done?"

"It's all right Chloe. You did what you had to do."

Her eyes closed. "Please, leave," she said, forcing the words out. "I don't know how much longer I can hold . . ."

"No." He was adamant. "We'll leave together or not at all."

The ground began to shake again as her eyes snapped open. Something that was not Chloe stared out at him, an alien presence.

"Chloe, come back to me my love."

A flicker, a glimmer. She was waging a silent war with whatever was trying to take possession of her. He took a step forward and she held up a hand in warning.

"No! Come no closer. I don't . . . I cannot control it." Her eyes went silver for a moment and he leaped back as she flung a line of pure energy in his direction.

He landed hard and rolled, ducking behind an empty container. "Chloe!" he shouted. "You have to fight it."

Energy streaked from her fingertips, blowing the canister away.

"Remember who you are," he shouted desperately. "You are Chloe. You are the one in control."

She was on her feet now.

"I . . . am . . . in control. I . . . am . . . my own . . . person. You cannot have me!"

Her eyes cleared and the glow faded. There was a moment of absolute quiet, then a building rumble. Chloe's face went ashen. "The pantarium," she whispered.

Zephryn got to his feet and went to her. "What about the pantarium?"

She was cold, so cold she thought she would never be warm again. "It's about to ignite."

He frowned. "But it's rock, isn't it? How is it possible to ignite it?"

"It's a very volatile rock, it's used to create fuel for ships." She clutched his arms as the ground heaved under their feet.

"Then we need to get out of here." He grabbed her by the hand and started leading her towards the cargo ship. Or tried to at least. Chloe dug her heels in to stop him.

"You don't understand. There's a huge deposit below us —"

"All the more reason to get out of here," he said, trying to tug her forward again.

"There's a series of deposits leading to the big one. It would only take one to start a chain reaction. If they should reach the big one . . ." she shuddered and swallowed hard.

"Granny was going to contact Martin to warn the other mines. With any luck they'll have already started to evacuate."

"It will blow this planet apart with such force . . . there will be no escape for anyone, even if they have enough warning to lift off."

"What can we do?"

"I don't know, I don't know. I can try and contain the smaller deposits, stabilize them, but I don't know if that'll be enough."

Zephryn felt a coldness filling his chest. Was this the great test Da'nat had talked about? If it was, it wasn't a fair one. Not by a long shot. "You have to try," he said. "I'll be right here with you."

She was already shaking her head. "No, if I fail—"

"If you fail then it won't matter where I am." He was still holding her hand and raised it to kiss her knuckles. "And if we are all to die then I would die with you."

Tears pricked at her eyes. "In saving the planet I might be taken over by the pantarium again and hurt you."

"It's a chance I'm willing to take."

She could see that he would not be swayed and it did something to her in the region of her heart. Unfortunately there was no time to argue. Chloe wanted to wrap herself around him, to sink herself into one of his fabulous kisses, but there was no time for that either.

"That ship is loaded with pantarium," she said, with a nod towards the cargo ship. "If you want to help, you need to get it out of here. If the pantarium inside it ignites then the explosion will trigger something I definitely won't be able to handle."

She lifted up for a quick kiss pressed to his lips, then she resolutely turned away. Once more she knelt on the ground, this time sinking her hands into the soil for a better connection.

Zephryn made a move as if to follow, but let her go. Instead he raced over to the open cargo ship and ducked inside. Once in the cockpit he perched on the edge of the pilot's seat and used one hand to begin a systems check and the other to seek the controls for closing the cargo bay doors.

If he had not spent a lifetime studying ships, he might have just locked everything down and used the manual controls to lift off. But the ship contained a sophisticated automated pilot system. He set the co-ordinates to take the ship on the most direct route out of the solar system he could find, and then set the automatic controls with a 20 second delay for lift off. That done, he headed back the way he'd come, sealing the hatch behind him.

There was nothing more he could do, it was all up to Chloe now.

* * * * *

As soon as she sensed the first of the ore start to become unstable, she surrounded it with earth, increasing the density to contain it. But the vibration set off the next one, and before it could be fully contained there was a whole chain of potential conflagrations. The ground undulated in reaction to it, fissures widening, new ones appearing. Setting off the main deposit of pantarium might not be the only problem they were facing here.

"There's a shelf," she said, sensing Zephryn's presence nearby. "Between the chain I'm keeping contained and the larger deposit."

"Can it be used to block it?"

"I don't know. I found it earlier and decided it was too dangerous so I went around it. This is my fault. I created a path. Had I not, the danger would have stopped at the shelf."

"You can't think like that. Could you close the path again?"

"I . . . I don't know. I can try."

Had the rock beneath them been porous, she doubted there was anything she could have done. But she was able to coax the loose soil and gravel, the rock that would only have been discarded, to fill the gaps she had left behind. It left gaps elsewhere, but far enough away from the pantarium deposits that it shouldn't matter.

The ground heaved beneath them. Zephryn fought to keep his footing, but Chloe was thrown to the side and lost her connection to the earth. She looked up at him.

"I was able to cut the smaller ones off from the main deposit, but there was a minor fault line . . . it's expanding and creating more cracks and fissures."

"What are you saying?"

"I'm saying that the planet's going to tear itself apart, and I am not strong enough to stop it."

Chapter Thirty-three

Zephryn helped Chloe to her feet and folded her in his arms for a quick hug.

"We need to get to the ship. We—"

She shook her head. "Even were we to reach it in time it wouldn't matter. The shockwave . . . there's no escape, we'd never get far enough away."

Zephryn's mind raced. It couldn't end like this. He didn't find Chloe just to lose her again, there had to be something they could do.

"What's causing fissures?" he asked.

"What?"

"What's making the fault lines expand, the fissures and cracks to widen?"

Chloe started to pull away from him. "Zephryn! We are about to die and you want a geology lesson?"

"Remember the volcano I spoke to you of? What saved us was a Fire Elemental. He drew the elemental energy from the lava, quenching the fire."

"Yes, I understand what you're saying." She cast her awareness along the widening fault lines. When an earthquake occurred, a certain amount of energy was released when the tectonic plates moved against each other. It was that energy that ripped the earth apart. It followed that if that energy was of the earth, she should be able to tap into it.

"I don't know . . ." There was so much power, more even than was put out by the pantarium. Chloe thought about all the people who would die if something wasn't done. Even those who made it to the ships in time would be in danger. She straightened her spine in determination. "I can try."

Moving a few steps away from Zephryn she stood with her head bowed, hands pointed towards the earth. "What did he do with the energy of the fire?" she asked, even as she reached for the energy of the earth.

Zephryn frowned. "He drew it into himself. But—"

Chloe was no longer listening. Her entire focus was on what was going on beneath their feet. The earth was shifting and although she could not stop it, she could draw on the energy the movement released to keep the damage at the minimum.

First she concentrated on the area surrounding the pantarium, keeping the deposits stable. If even one of them was set off they were doomed. Then she went beyond it, deeper towards the planet's heart to keep the crust around the molten core intact. This was key to keeping the planet from breaking apart. Once she started to draw the energy into herself she found it easy, far too easy.

Cracks and fissures still radiated outwards, but the catastrophic damage they should have caused was minimized. There was still damage, far too much damage. The earth still heaved and sank along the fault lines. Mines collapsed and towns were swallowed whole, but the planet itself began to stabilize.

The energy was like a living thing inside her. She fought to stay in control, to retain her "self". Zephryn was forced to take a step back as the energy began to manifest physically.

"I can't hold it," she said, her voice frightened. "It burns!"

Zephryn stared at her helplessly. *Da'nat! Help us!*

We come.

Part of him hoped they'd be bringing the ship with them so they could escape this place, but another part of him hoped Da'nat used whatever transport device that was used on him earlier. Time was running out for them.

Green and brown, and every colour in between, lines of energy began licking over Chloe's form. Zephryn summoned a cooling wind and spun it around her, trying desperately to keep her from burning up.

The ground beneath them quieted, but still the energy within Chloe built. She was unable to talk, only feel. The earth's energy was consuming her from within. She didn't know how much longer she was going to be able to hold it before it exploded outward.

Zephryn's scout ship landed in almost the same place the cargo ship had been. Both Granny and Da'nat joined Zephryn where he stood.

"I'm sorry, this is my fault," he told them. "I told her about how Pyre was able to draw the Elemental Fire into himself to stop the volcano. Now she's done the same with the energy from the earth."

"Chloe, can you hear me child?" Granny asked, taking a step towards her.

"What's . . . happening to me?"

"You have done what Pyrphoros did - you have taken your element's energy into yourself. Now you must do as he did and release it."

"I don't . . ." she sobbed and fell to her knees. "I can't!"

Da'nat held Zephryn back when he would have gone to her. "You cannot help her."

"You can do this!" Granny said fiercely. "Release it, now!"

Chloe threw back her head and screamed as she was enveloped in a swirling column of green and brown energy. It shot straight upwards into space. It seemed to go on forever, but was gone in an instant. Her eyes rolled back in her head as she slid bonelessly to the ground.

"Fire and water," Granny whispered. "Earth and air."

* * * * *

Zephryn jerked away from Da'nat and went to kneel down beside Chloe. Unsure if it was safe to touch her. He looked up at Da'nat, but Da'nat was focused on Granny.

"What did you mean," Da'nat said to her. "Fire and water, earth and air?"

"It was our doing," she said in a wondering tone of voice. "All our doing. Had we not meddled in that which we should not, none of this would have come to pass."

"What's she talking about?" Zephryn asked.

Da'nat hesitated. "I believe events have led to the unbalancing of her mind .She but speaks nonsense. Do not fear, it is safe to touch her," he said with a gesture towards Chloe.

Zephryn gingerly gathered Chloe in his arms. When nothing

untoward happened, he held her more closely and rose to her feet.

"We should leave this place," Da'nat said, laying a hand on Granny's shoulder. "You must come with us."

She stirred and looked at him, eyes glassy.

"I was not meant to survive."

"But you did. And now your people have need of your wisdom."

"My people." She gave a sharp laugh. "I do not even know who they are any more."

"Then you will learn," Da'nat said gently, leading her into the ship. Zephryn followed behind, hitting the hatch control as he passed it, sealing the ship.

Da'nat led an unresisting Granny to the lounge and seated her in one of the chairs. Zephryn followed in their wake, unsure what to do with Chloe.

Da'nat turned towards him. "Though it will be some time before she recovers, she is in no immediate danger. A bed should suffice for her recovery."

"But she will recover, right?" Zephryn was not ashamed that he needed the Ilezie's reassurance.

"Yes."

He nodded and carried Chloe to his quarters, making her as comfortable as possible on his own bed. He lingered, brushing a hand over her hair before turning and heading to the bridge.

Da'nat was already there, in his customary seat. Before going through the instrument check, Zephryn turned on the scanners. It appeared that the danger was over - the seismic activity had all but stopped. The planet was stabilizing again.

"Do you think Martin was able to warn the other mines in time?" he asked.

"I do not know. I believe . . ."

Zephryn turned to look at him. It was unlike the Ilezie to leave a thought unfinished.

"Even if he did, there is no way of knowing whether they listened to him or not. If they did not, then the casualties will be high."

Zephryn turned back to the controls, running through the lift off protocols. Once they'd cleared the planet's atmosphere he had another question.

"Do you think the survivors will rebuild?"

"It is doubtful. This planet was close to being mined out."

"In that case, there's a cargo ship full of pantarium in orbit. I think we should contact Martin - I think he can be trusted to distribute the wealth fairly."

"That is a noble gesture. I concur."

Zephryn sent out the call and in a short time made contact with Martin. The miners had not gone far, rendezvousing at a mutually agreed upon point. Martin was all but speechless when he was told of the pantarium. It was a blessing for the group, who had lost pretty much everything but the clothes on their backs.

"So now what," Zephryn asked, itching to go check on Chloe.

"Set the co-ordinates to zero-alpha-alpha-seven," Da'nat told him.

"And this will take us . . . where?" he asked, laying in the course.

"On the way to completing our mission," Da'nat told him.

Zephryn turned to look at him. "But . . . I thought . . ."

"At this point we need only to confirm the trajectory of the energy beam."

"But we already know its trajectory."

"Perhaps," Da'nat said enigmatically.

Zephryn sighed, knowing there was no point in trying to get any more information out of the Ilezie.

"Course laid in," he said. He set the automatic controls and rose from his seat. "I'm going to check on Chloe." He turned at the door. "But when I come back, you and I are going to have a long over-due talk.

* * * * *

Zephryn smoothed a hand over Chloe's hair. There was no change in her condition. Despite Da'nat's assurances she'd be fine, he used a portable medical scanner on her. He was by no means an expert at interpreting the readings, but it appeared there was nothing seriously wrong with her. As Da'nat said, she just needed rest.

Covering her with a light blanket, left his quarters in search of the Ilezie. He found him in the lounge with Granny, who was looking only slightly better than she had been.

"When was the last time you ate?" Granny asked him.

He blinked in confusion. "I . . . that would have been early this morning, with Chloe."

"Sit and eat, and I will answer your questions."

Zephryn hesitated for a long moment in the doorway before going to the food processor and programming a meal. When it finished cycling through its program, he carried the tray to the small table near the view port.

"How did you get the ship unburied without Chloe's help?"

Da'nat made as if to answer but she shook her head at him. "The boy's done well. He deserves the truth."

"I am not without power, you've sensed that. I merely used some to free the ship."

"You're an Earth Elemental? Like Chloe and her mother?" He frowned. "But why keep it a secret from them? You—"

"I am not an Ardraci, nor am I an elemental. I am . . . something else."

"What?"

"I do not know any more," she said sadly.

Chapter Thirty-four

Chloe awoke slowly, with no idea of where she was or what had happened. There was softness beneath her, and blankets weighing her down. A bed then, someplace safe because there was a warmth along one side of her.

Her memory began to slowly return, but it was more like a dream, the images that filtered through her mind. Flashes really - shooting stars, a beautiful man from space, a mine collapsing, brilliantly coloured flowers . . .

She came fully awake with a gasp, sitting up in the bed. Her actions woke the person who'd been sleeping beside her. Chloe was breathing heavily as she stared at Zephryn, trying to make sense of things. He stared back at her, as though waiting for something.

"We're alive!" she blurted.

A smile blossomed on his face. "Yes, we are."

"But . . . how?"

He sat up beside her and pulled her over for a kiss. "You drew the earth energy into yourself and stabilized the planet. You saved us all."

"Oh." For a moment she was content to just rest in his arms, enjoying his warmth and the fact they were safe, and together. Then her head popped up off of his shoulder.

"Where are we? Where's my mother? Is she safe? What—"

Zephryn heaved a sigh, then placed his fingers over her mouth to stop her questions. "I was told you'd be hungry when you woke up. Let's get something to eat and I'll explain everything."

He snagged a pair of robes from a chair beside the bed. Passing one over to her, he donned the other himself. Extending his hand, he helped her from the bed, pulling her into his arms to steal another kiss. "But we're going to be finishing this later."

"Deal," she said with a grin. Belting her own robe tightly, she followed him out of the bedroom and into a spacious sitting room with a round table on one side and a pair of couches with matching chairs grouped together on the other side.

"Where are we?" she asked, looking around curiously. It was a pleasant room, but a little sterile looking. There was a large window on the wall closest to the couches and through it she could see . . . "Stars?" she asked, taking a step closer.

"Come and sit down," he told her, guiding her gently to a seat at the table.

With effort she bit back her questions and watched as he went over to a panel in the wall. Her eyebrows rose as he typed something into a keypad and the panel slid open to expose a platter of food.

"That's a food dispenser," he told her, setting the platter on the table between them. "It can be programmed to make just about any food you could possibly want."

She nodded to show she heard him. This was starting to become a little overwhelming. Reaching for the earth to ground herself, her eyes widened in fear.

"It's gone! I can no longer feel the earth!" Tears filled her eyes. "I must have burned out my gift at the end."

He was at her side in an instant, holding her in his comforting arms. "No, my love. You're fine. We're on a starship, that's all. There just aren't any planets close enough for you to connect to."

"A ship?" She snuffled against him. "We're on your ship?"

"Not my ship," he said with a chuckle, releasing her again. "Now eat."

Dutifully she picked at the food he'd ordered up for them.

"We're aboard the *Valkyrie*, the ship my ship came from."

"And my mother?" She was almost afraid to ask.

"She's safe, she's fine. She's in the medical bay. I'll take you to see her later. The doctors say with time she'll make a full recovery."

"Oh, Zephryn!"

"Keep eating," he ordered.

"How long was I unconscious?" Her appetite was coming back, now that she knew her mother was safe.

"More than a week," he said soberly.

Chloe choked on her mouthful of food.

"When you collapsed . . . I thought I'd lost you," he said quietly. "I've never been so scared in all my life."

"I wish I could describe what it was like . . . I—" She reached out and touched the back of his hand. "At first it was euphoric, like joining with the pantarium, only more intense. It wasn't until I tried to fight it that I felt the pain. It was like a fire burning inside of me. And when I released all that energy into space . . ." Shaking her head she looked out at the stars.

Zephryn looked like there was something he wanted to get off his chest, but wasn't sure if he should or not.

"What is it?" she asked.

Still he hesitated. "I never told you what we were doing in the badlands, did I?"

She shook her head. "Just something about a scientific expedition."

"Remember I told you about the volcano, and how Pyre, the Fire Elemental, pulled the energy into himself?"

"The same thing I did."

"Pyre had trouble controlling his gift, and began pulling energy from the planet's core. By the time he was able to stop himself, he'd built up an incredible amount. He released it into space as well, where it kept traveling. We were following it and got too close it—I don't know how else to put it, it lashed out, causing us to crash on Belspar."

Chloe gave up even the pretence of eating. "And the energy I released?"

"It merged with it. The thing is, it's not just fire and earth energy. Other elementals tried to contain the fire energy with wind and water. And your energy drew on the energy from the wind I had created to cool you down."

"So this . . . mass of energy is formed from all four elements?"

"Yes."

She thought about it for a moment. "I wonder if anything like it has ever happened before."

"I don't know. I can't help feeling it has greater significance than we know, but nobody seems to want to talk about it."

"If it could cause a ship passing too close to it to crash, what would happen if it passed too close to a world?"

"I don't even want to think about the damage it could do," he admitted. "We calculated the new trajectory of it and as far as I could determine it's not going to pass close to any settled worlds. Or even unsettled ones for that matter."

Chloe glanced towards the view port and shivered. "I think whatever it is, we are not done with it yet. Nor it with us."

"Having a premonition?" Zephryn asked.

"No just a feeling."

He directed a smouldering stare at her. "I have to admit I'm having a feeling myself. Care to guess what it is?"

She met his stare with a mischievous grin. "Would it have something to do with the softness of the bed in the other room?"

"It might."

"Then perhaps that is one mystery we might solve together."

His eyes lit up. "It would be my pleasure."

"Hopefully not all your pleasure," Chole told him, pushing away from the table. "Race you!"

Zephryn didn't need his wind to lend wings to his feet.

#

About the Author

Carol R. Ward began with the belief she was meant to be a writer of short stories, however her stories tended to be rather long. They also tended to have a romantic thread running through them. Finally caving in to the inevitable, she embraced her genre and began writing novels of fantasy/science fiction adventure with a dash of romance thrown into the mix. She has never regretted it.

Living with her husband and four cats in Cobourg, Ontario, she writes a variety of prose: non-fiction, flash fiction, short stories, and novels – in a variety of genres: humour, horror, contemporary, romance, science fiction, and fantasy. She's also a prolific poet.

You can visit Carol on her blog at: My Writing Journal (http://rightwriterright.blogpot.com). She can also be found as Carol R. Ward on Facebook (https://www.facebook.com/Carol-R-Ward-Author-308347952512637/) and CarolRWard on Twitter (https://twitter.com/CarolRWard).

She loves to hear from her fans and you can email her directly at: crward.author@gmail.com

Other Books by the Author

The Moonstone Chronicles
Magical Misfire
Lucky Dog

The Ardraci Elementals
An Elemental Wind
An Elemental Fire
An Elemental Water